RACHEL CORD
Confidential Investigations

Where The Hell Is Tessa Ryker?

R. E. Conary

Everyone Deserves An Equal Footing

Where The Hell Is Tessa Ryker?
RACHEL CORD
Confidential Investigations
Book Five

Copyright © 2020 R. E. Conary
Cover Art © www.gograph.com/Tawng

Equal Footing Books
ISBN: 978-1946545046

Prologue

Gunshots broke Tessa's reverie. She turned seeking the source of the sound. It seemed close and yet far enough away that it didn't scare the birds or squirrels in the trees above her. The sound confused her. Where? Muffled somehow. Hunters? Shouldn't be. Dad didn't allow hunting on their land. Who would fire a gun here? We don't own guns.

Another muffled gunshot. Tessa looked up the hill. The sound came from the direction of their house. Why? Who? She raced up the trail from the creek. There shouldn't be gunshots coming from her home. There shouldn't!

The white peak of their farmhouse against the cloudless, azure sky came into view across the wide, stubbled field as she neared the edge of the woods. When she saw their covered front porch, she heard one more gunshot coming from the house. Tessa froze in the shadows of the trees. She fell to the ground shaking not sure what frightened her.

Moments later, a man stepped out of the house to the edge of the porch. She was too far away to recognize him but knew it wasn't her father. He wore tannish pants and a dark brown, long-sleeved shirt. He looked back toward the door then pounded the porch column. He leaned against the column, his face buried against his arm, for nearly a minute. He straightened and scanned the horizon, the sun glinting from mirrored sunglasses and from something shiny on his chest and on his collar. As his head swiveled toward her, Tessa crouched further into the shadows. Who was he? Did he have something to do with the gunshots?

The man stood gazing for several moments and looked back briefly at the front door one last time. He wiped at something on his sleeve and the front of his shirt. He wiped his hand on his trousers. He stepped off the porch putting on a brown Stetson and walked to a white SUV. Now Tessa saw the heavy gun belt he wore, recognized the shiny thing on his chest as a badge and realized he was from the sheriff's department.

What were those shots? What happened? Was he leaving or calling for help? She heard the SUV start, watched it turn in the yard and drive away. Tessa gaped when she saw it was Blank County Sheriff Baxter Donahue's official Ford Explorer. She'd seen him in it many times. Sheriff Donahue?

Tessa wasn't sure how long she sat at the edge of the woods. Total fear gripped her. Played games with her mind. The dust raised by the SUV on the long dirt drive to the road had blown away before she was able to think—to approach the house.

The sharp smell of gunpowder invaded her senses as she entered. Before she could make sense of what she smelled or her eyes adjusted from the outside brightness, she covered her mouth in horror as she saw legs in the dim hallway. Her mother lay face down as if fleeing. Blood splattered the hall wall and puddled about her mother's head. Tessa gagged. Turned away.

Her father lay crumpled on the living room floor. Part of his head was blown away. In his left hand was a black handgun like those Tessa had seen in movies and on television. Sour acid rose in her throat. She turned and rushed through the dining room and kitchen to avoid the horror of her mother's body on the hallway floor, her father in the living room. She ran to the hall bathroom, to the toilet and vomited. Kept vomiting until only acid scorched her throat.

Still gagging, she rinsed her mouth at the sink. The face that stared back at her in the mirror was wide-eyed and pale.

Mom? Dad? What happened here? What . . . Trina! Where's Trina?

Tessa ran to her sister's bedroom. Trina wasn't in bed as she should be. She'd been sick that morning and feverish. Mom had kept her home from school. Where was she? Had she heard the shots? Seen what . . .? She wasn't under the bed or in the closet or in Tessa's room or their parents' room or bathroom. Where could she be?

Tessa ran back to the kitchen hoping Trina had run out the back. Had gotten away. Prayed she hadn't seen . . . The kitchen door was closed. Tessa opened it but the screen door was latched. Where would Trina hide? The pantry door was partly open.

"Trina? Are you in there? It's okay. It's Tessa."

Trina lay on the pantry floor like a pile of rags. Tessa couldn't see her face. It was buried in her arms the way she would do it when she didn't want to be seen.

Tessa reached out. "Trina? Are you okay?"

She touched Trina's slack and cooling arm. Her sister didn't move. She ran back to the bathroom and dry heaved into the toilet. Her stomach, throat and lungs burned. Shaking, she knelt by the toilet no longer able to stand. She sat on the floor and cried.

Time passed. Tessa's face was wet. She wiped at her face smearing it and her hand with tears and snot. She grabbed a hand towel to clean her face and hand. Eyes still streaming, Tessa forced herself up and returned to the kitchen. She sat in the pantry doorway numbly leaning against the frame. She couldn't look at her sister but pulled one of Trina's arms free and held her hand.

Why? How did this happen? She remembered the gun in her father's hand. Dad? What did you . . .? Need to call 911.

Tessa pulled out her cellphone to punch in the numbers. She stopped. Oh, God! Sheriff Donahue. Why was he here? He was in the house when . . . Why did he leave? Why didn't he stay and help? Call an ambulance? Why did he . . .?

Minutes passed. Tessa blankly looked around the kitchen trying to absorb what happened to her family. Her eyes fell on the wall clock: 1:22.

I'm not supposed to be here. I should be in Mrs. Powers English class. The bus. I don't get home until four. If I hadn't skipped, hadn't been down by the creek eating my heart out over Brian, I wouldn't have found this—them—Mom, Dad, Trina—not until I came . . . Oh, God! What am I going to do?

Tessa shook uncontrollably. Minutes passed before she was calm enough to think.

Where'd that gun come from? We don't have guns. Why does Dad have it? Why would he kill us? It makes no sense. Dad wouldn't do this. He couldn't. He didn't.

The sheriff? He must have brought the gun. But why would the sheriff . . .? Why was he here? Did he . . .? Oh, God. He did it. He must have killed them. I can't call 911. If I do, he'll know I'm here. Know I must have seen—

Tessa looked at her dead sister. "Oh, Trina. I'm so sorry. I love you."

She ran to her bedroom. Pulled out her pink sports bag. Threw clothes into it. Grabbed her laptop and stuffed it in the bag. Added her cellphone charger. Took her parka from the closet. Opened the music box she'd gotten for her eighth birthday, took out the $45 she'd saved and stuffed it into her jeans.

Have to get away. The sheriff will find out I wasn't in school. He'll know I was here. He'll find me. Kill me too.

She went to her parents' bedroom. Sorry, Mom. She opened her mother's purse and wallet and took all the cash. Eighty-three dollars. She hesitated then took a credit card and her mother's driver's license. From a bottom dresser drawer, hidden beneath sweaters, she took a small metal box containing emergency cash, birth certificates, her father's

Army records and insurance papers and put it in her bag. She went back to the kitchen. Stroked her dead sister's cheek.

"He won't get away with this, Trina. I promise you. I won't let him get away with it. I'll prove he did this. Somehow I'll prove it."

Tessa took the keys to her father's crewcab from the hook by the kitchen door. She opened the door and stopped. Dropped her bag and went back and looked at her mom in the hallway. There was so much blood on the floor she couldn't go to her without stepping in it.

"I love you, Mom."

She went back through the kitchen and the dining room to the living room where her father lay crumpled in front of his favorite chair. She looked down at her father. Closed her eyes for a moment. More tears wetted her cheeks. Looked at the gun in his hand. She shook her head.

"He screwed up, didn't he, Dad?"

Tessa took a deep breath then used her phone to take a picture of her father's body. She took a close-up of the gun in his left hand. She saved the photos to her cloud memory.

Yeah. He screwed up. Big time. You're left-handed but you're right-eyed. You aim with your right eye and always shot right-handed when we had guns. I remember that when you taught me to shoot. Taught me how to determine my dominant eye. The sheriff should have remembered that. He was your friend. Knew you most of your life. You were together in the Guard. Others will remember it, though. They'll know he screwed up.

"We'll get him, Dad. I'll get him."

Tessa glanced at the photograph on the table that separated her parents' chairs. The picture was three years old. It had been taken at the county fair. Her mom, dad, Trina and she sat on hay bales arms around each other smiling at the camera. Trina held a small stuffed bear Dad won at the ring toss booth.

Tessa wiped tears from her eyes. She turned to leave but stopped. She turned back and took the gun from her father's hand.

"This way the sheriff can't spin the blame on you, Dad. They can't be sure what really happened. They'll have to investigate. He made mistakes. Probably made others that someone will catch. He won't get away with it. I won't let him. I love you, Dad."

Tessa used a kitchen towel to wipe off her father's fingerprints and wrap the gun in. She put it in her bag and went out the door to her father's truck. She tossed the bag on the floor, put the key in the ignition, sat back biting her lip to keep from crying, from falling apart completely.

You taught me to drive, Dad. Not old enough for a permit yet, but you taught me anyway. Just like you taught me to drive the tractor, the field truck and the harvester. Now she smiled. Your *little harvester*. That's what you called me. Remember? Because that was one meaning of my name.

Well, another is *reaper*. And that's what I'm going to do, Dad. Reap Sheriff Donahue's ass.

I don't understand. Why would he do this, Dad? Thought he was your friend. Our friend. He's had dinner with us many times. Treated Trina to rides in his SUV with the siren going. You were in high school together. The same Guard unit. You were together in Afghanistan when you got wounded, weren't you? So why, Dad? Why?

Tessa remembered when her father came home four years ago. He'd been wounded by an IED on patrol. Spent ten months in an Army hospital in Germany recovering. When he came home he took a medical discharge and got rid of all the guns in the house. Said he didn't want to play war no more. Didn't want to shoot anything ever again. He never said why or what happened over there but still took medication for nightmares that haunted him. His screams often woke Tessa in the middle of the night. She'd listen to his sobs as Mom tried to calm him. He still went monthly to the VA medical center in Omaha for therapy.

The farm had suffered the year-and-a-half he was away. Just Mom with Trina at her hip, Tessa and occasional migrant workers to keep things going as best they could. The bills piling up when they couldn't get enough for the few crops they harvested to break even. Her mother never said anything. Just kept going waiting for Dad to get well and come home. When he finally returned, things got better. That's when he taught her to drive the farm equipment. The farm flourished again. He got top dollar for their crops. There was money for the bills, for extras, for . . .

Tessa remembered one night shortly after her father came home. She couldn't sleep. She heard the kitchen screen door squeak and went to her bedroom window. Watched her father carry a duffel bag to the barn. Curious, she sneaked out to see. Watched him hide it. Had seen him go there other times after that. Usually after the crops had been sold or a large bill needed to be paid.

What was in that duffel, Dad? Was it still there? Tessa got out of the truck and went to the barn. Went to the tool room, and like she'd watched her father years ago, she moved boxes and lifted out floorboards. In a cubbyhole beneath the floor was an Army duffel bag with his name and service number stamped on it. She pulled it out. It looked less bulky than she remembered. A padlock kept it closed. She remembered the small key on her father's keyring. Went and got it from the truck.

The bag was filled with loose cash. How much Tessa had no idea. Must be thousands.

Where did you get this, Dad? Is this where all the extras came from? Not from selling the crops? But why hide it? Why isn't it in the bank? Is this stolen money? From Afghanistan? You and the sheriff were over there together. Did the two of you . . . Is this what he wants? Why he killed you and Mom and Trina? For this?

Tessa wanted to hide the bag again or — better yet — burn it. Then she realized she'd need money. A lot more than she already had. Money to live on. Money to prove the sheriff's guilt. She closed the hole and moved the boxes back. Shouldered the bag and returned to the truck.

She thought of the gun. What if it were found near Sheriff Donahue's house? Could he explain that? Wouldn't that make him the suspect? Tessa shook her head. I'd have to drive through Hartfield to get there. Go right past the courthouse and sheriff's office. What if someone sees me? What if *he* sees me?

Tessa looked at the truck's clock. A little after two. She needed to be far away before the sheriff became suspicious she hadn't reported her parents' murder. When she reached the road, she turned south away from town.

He looked at his watch for the umpteenth time: 5:45. Nervously drummed his fingers on his desk. Normally, on a quiet day like this, he'd be headed home before now. Getting ready to sit down to dinner with his wife and children. But he'd waited. Pretended to work on reports that could easily wait until morning. Waited for that emergency call he knew would come. Had to come. Should have come already.

Fuck. The girl had to be home by now. School's been out for hours. Why hasn't she called for help? Where is she? He went down the hall to the dispatcher's room.

"Anything happening?"

"Pretty quiet, sir. You working late?"

"Paperwork. Never gets done. So, nothing happening?"

"Not really. Harvey's giving a speeding ticket to Martin Kline out on Route 75. That's the third time this fall already. Bet his insurance is gonna get hiked. That's about all the excitement we've got, and I pray it stays that way."

"Me too. Thanks, Beth. I'm headed home. If anything important comes up don't hesitate to call."

"Yes, sir. Good night."

He continued down the hall and went out the employee entrance to his personal car. Sat thinking. *Where could she be? Why hasn't she called? Hasn't she gone home? Should I go out there and check? No. Better not. What reason could I give? Shit! Where is she?*

Calm. Stay calm. Think it out. There was no one else there. No witnesses. No one stopped out at the road curious of hearing shots. It'll look like Terry did it. Wherever the girl is, she'll show up and report it. Just have to wait till she does. No need for panic. Have to get rid of that bloody uniform, though. That's my first priority. He sat back closing his eyes, breathing slowly, trying to be calm.

He slammed the steering wheel. *Damn it! Why didn't Terry just give me the money for Christ's sake? Tell me where he hid it? It's mine as much as his. We found it together, damn it. I got it back here. I should have had a bigger share. Why, Terry? Why did you have to grab the gun? Fuck! I was just trying to scare you. Make you understand how bad I need that money right now. And Caroline. Oh, shit. And the little girl . . . Katrina? Is that her name? Why did she have to be home?*

He beat the wheel. *Fuck! Fuck! Fuck! Where the hell is Tessa Ryker?*

One

"Calvin, fuck the—"

I woke with a start, sitting up, breathing heavily, covered in sweat. Had I screamed? Wendy still slept undisturbed beside me. I breathed slowly to calm myself. Looked at the clock: 4:47. Too damn early. The sun wouldn't be up for hours but I couldn't fall back asleep. Not after that.

Easing out of bed, I picked up my robe, quietly closed the bedroom door and went to the kitchen. My breathing was normal but I was shaking and anxious as I opened the cupboard door. I looked at the bottles of pills for my PTSD. It'd been 15 years since I was tortured and raped and killed Gwen Archer and Calvin Tierney in self-defense, but there were still moments when they returned to haunt me.

I stared at the bottles for several minutes then closed the cupboard. Probably out of date, anyway. Couldn't recall the last time I took them. I opened another cupboard, took down the bottle of Glenfiddich and half-filled a tumbler. "Use what works," that's my mantra. Tastes better too. I opened the vertical blinds to the sliding glass doors to our balcony, turned a comfortable chair around, sat in the dark and stared at the wide river and the reflection of lights on the water from the city on the other side, waited for the sun and sipped my pacifier.

The river flowed before me unseeing, uncaring; oblivious to what lay buried in its muck and mired bottom or to what churned in the muck and mire of my mind. I've made many mistakes, have a lifetime of regrets, but that night at Calvin Tierney's across the river plagues me more than others.

I'd been looking for a 14-year-old runaway—Linda Miller—who'd reminded me a lot of a younger me. I thought I'd find information to help me at Tierney's. Hadn't expected to find her there—held captive. Hadn't thought I needed backup that night or let anyone know where I was going. Had to be the Lone Ranger. Hadn't expected the psychotically vicious vengeance of Archer when she and Tierney caught me helping Miller escape.

I shivered. The memory rose from the muck threatening to overwhelm me again. I gulped the Scotch and stared oblivious, unseeing, uncaring at the passing river.

A hand on my shoulder woke me. Bright sunshine made me wince, but its warmth through the windows felt good.

"Bad night?"

I looked at the empty tumbler in my hand then up to Wendy's worried face.

"Nightmare. I'm okay now."

"Are you sure? You haven't had one in a long time. Should we call Natalie?"

"No. If I have more, I'll call. Make an appointment to see her. Promise. Stop worrying. What time is it?"

"Just after eight."

I stood. "Better get moving. I've a 9 o'clock client."

Doris Garrity was at the round reception desk as I topped the second floor stairs to the west wing of Mann Avenue Plaza.

"Good morning, Rachel. Your nine o'clock was early, but Barb was here. She took him down to your offices."

"Thanks, Doris."

Offices still sounded strange to me. Mann Avenue Plaza was an old high school renovated for small businesses. Up until two years ago, my *office* was one half of one of the larger classrooms on the second floor that had been divided for additional office space. It had always been big enough for my one-woman agency. When the other half became available, Doris and Mary Farr, who provide secretarial services for me as well as most of the other small businesses on the second floor, convinced me it was time for expansion. Office expansion led to agency expansion, which led me to convince Barbara Lange to become an investigator and work with me.

When we first met, Barbara was a smartass 14-year-old with ink-black hair and purple lips wearing a crotch-length red sheath. Back then Barbara helped me find the runaway Linda Miller and, a few months later, I rescued Barb from the clutches of a pedophile. Since then, she did some growing up and graduated with a bachelor's degree from the University of Illinois in Social Work with a minor in Criminology and Criminal Justice. Her first job was as a juvenile probation officer in Springfield, Illinois. We kept in touch and Barb always seemed more interested in my stories than hers, so it wasn't too hard to convince her to join me. Besides, getting a PI license here is easier than in Illinois.

As our client had already arrived, I passed my old office entrance—which now said *Private*—to the new entry of Confidential Investigations.

Barb was seated in the sitting area in a smart navy business suit and cream blouse. Her long, light brown hair arranged in a braided updo. Across from her sat a ruggedly tanned man— obviously our client—mid to late forties like me, wearing a worn leather bomber, pressed jeans, buffed Tony Lama's, a blue broadcloth shirt and crimson knit tie with a sheriff's badge tiebar. Coffee, a plate of assorted donuts and Barb's iPad were on the low table between them. A brown, straw Stetson lay atop a thick file folder on the seat beside the man. They both rose. He was at least 6'3" in his boots.

"Good morning. I'm Rachel Cord. Sorry I wasn't here to greet you."

I reached out and shook his calloused, firm and dry hand.

"How do, ma'am. No problem at all. I'm a bit early. Miss Lange made me welcome. I'm Sheriff Baxter Donahue from Blank County, Nebraska. Pleased to meet you."

His gravelly voice reminded me of actor Sam Elliott which made me like him right off. Too bad he didn't have the 'stache.

"Call me, Rachel. Only school children call me ma'am. Please sit."

"Thank you, ma'am — Rachel."

As we sat, my stomach rumbled reminding me that in my rush to be on time, I'd skipped breakfast. I covetously eyed the donuts before turning to my client.

"I'm a little surprised you're a law officer, Sheriff Donahue. That wasn't mentioned when the appointment was made. I was told I'd be looking for a runaway teen. Are you related or is this part of an official investigation?"

"Not exactly related. Tessa's dad was a close friend and colleague."

"Tessa?"

"Tessa Ryker. The missing girl I'd like you to find. She's fourteen. And, yes, it is part of an ongoing investigation."

"How so?"

Sheriff Donahue pursed his lips seeming to give thought to how he was going to answer. I doubted he had much experience briefing private investigators. He sighed and looked me straight in the eye.

"Two weeks ago, October eighth, Terry Ryker, Tessa's father, her mother Caroline and her sister Katrina were murdered in their home outside Hartfield and Tessa went missing."

"Is she suspected of killing her family?"

"There is some conjecture along those lines. The deaths weren't reported until the next day. At first, we thought she might be dead too, but when we didn't find a body we thought she'd been kidnapped. Ryker's F-150 was missing and we didn't find the murder weapon. We thought the girl too young to drive. Thought someone else must have been there and taken her or she went with that person willingly. We just don't know—aren't sure—how she's involved. We immediately put out an APB on the truck and the girl to neighboring states. We were already a day late, but it was all we could do at the time. Your police department notified us when they found the truck a few days ago and reported that Tessa was seen here. She may only be a witness that managed to get away from her abductor, but some think she did it. Why is anyone's guess. Won't know—can't know—what really happened until we talk with her. Thing is, she hasn't called or contacted anyone we know of. Not us or any other authority either."

"This is new for me, Sheriff. Law enforcement doesn't usually come knocking for my help."

He smiled. "Can't say I've had much use—or desire, beggin' your pardon—for private help before, but then again, I'm not used to homicide in my county, much less a triple homicide. Thing is, I need to find Tessa Ryker, and I'm willing to think outside the box to do it."

"And you think she's here?"

"Just my feeling. She's young. Has to be scared near to death. For some reason feels she needs to hide. This is a big city and easy for someone to get lost in or hide in, as I understand."

"That's very true."

"And I'm given to understand that you're known for locating runaways."

"That's true too. Who told you about me?"

"Lieutenant Brody from Central Division Homicide."

"I've known Denise a long time. We traded information often when she was with Missing Persons. When was Tessa seen here?"

"Unfortunately, October eighth. Same day as the murders. Late night at the Greyhound station. Late enough that she could have driven here after the murders. Your police didn't know this until after they found the truck three days ago. A patrol spotted the truck and pulled it over and arrested the guy driving it. He said he found it a block from the bus station early morning October tenth unlocked with the key in the ignition. He decided to 'borrow it' in his own words and has been using it to haul stuff. The man has alibis for the days before and following the murders. He was nowhere near Nebraska. Police searched his place just in case but found nothing else linking him to Tessa Ryker.

"As the guy found it close by, the police checked with Greyhound. A ticket agent remembered a young girl wanting a ticket late October eighth. The agent didn't believe the girl was eighteen and asked for ID. When the girl said she had none, the agent asked if she were a runaway and wanted to go home. Said their Home Free program could provide a free ticket. The girl got nervous and left before the agent could summon help. When shown a picture, the agent was almost sure it was Tessa Ryker. She'd put her hair up in a bun and was wearing black-framed glasses to look older. Surveillance cameras caught her coming and going from the station but not where she went. That's the last verified sighting of her, I'm afraid."

"Two weeks is a lot of time to get lost. Do you know where she was trying to go?"

"Seattle, Washington, according to the ticket agent. She has an aunt out there so that makes sense. Mrs. Rebecca Wilson. I spoke with her as Caroline Ryker's next of kin. She's an older sister. As Terry had no relatives, Mrs. Wilson is currently in Hartfield to handle the funerals. Those are planned this coming Monday. I spoke with her again when I heard Tessa could be headed to Seattle. She called her husband but no one's heard from the girl."

I shook my head in thought. "If she eluded a kidnapper, why hasn't she called you or the police here?"

"That's my first question too."

"And if she wasn't kidnapped, why didn't she head for Seattle first rather than here? We're in the wrong direction. She obviously had money for gas if she could buy a bus ticket. Any relatives or close friends here?"

"None that we know of. Can't explain why she came here or if she is still here."

"Maybe she's hitchhiking and is long gone," Barb suggested. "She knows now she can't buy a bus or train ticket because of her age and without ID. She probably knew the police would look for the truck. Dump it and get out of town as fast as you can."

I looked at her. "She's fourteen. Would she think of something like that?"

Barb smiled. "I would have. Anyone over five watching TV knows about APBs and BOLOs. Getting rid of the truck would be an automatic reaction for anyone wanting to hide. And she was smart enough to leave the keys in it."

She had me there. Sometimes I forget how aware kids are.

"So we don't know if she's here or on her way to Seattle or somewhere else entirely. Does she have a cellphone you can locate?"

"She did." Donahue actually chuckled. "That was our first wild goose chase."

"How so?"

"Once we found out she had a phone, we got warrants and contacted her provider. That took a lot longer than I liked, but we finally tracked the phone's GPS history to El Paso."

"Texas?"

"One and the same. The GPS history showed she was home at the time of the murders and phone records pinged her near Nebraska City about three p.m. that day. Then the phone went dead. Figured she turned it off. At five o'clock it was active again and the GPS history said she was at the welcome center on I-29 near Rock Port. When we were able to check security footage at the center, it showed her there alone. If she'd been kidnapped, she could have asked anyone then for help but didn't. From there GPS tracked the phone to El Paso where it went dead again at two forty-five a.m., October eleventh. We notified the El Paso police as soon as we found out, and they went to the home where it was last located early the next morning."

"And?"

"The family that lived there never knew of or ever met Tessa Ryker."

"But?"

"Yes, but." Donahue smiled. "The family's oldest son drove home from Minneapolis and made a pit stop at the Rock Port welcome center around five p.m. on the eighth. He was there maybe a half hour or so. The El Paso police searched and found the dead phone wedged between his truck's cab and toolbox. The young man remembered parking next to a white Ford SuperCrew. Remembered it because it was a lot newer than the truck he was driving. It was gone when he came back from the restroom and getting snacks from the vending machines. He didn't remember seeing a teenage girl there though."

"Clever girl." I ignored Barb's grin.

Donahue nodded. "Definitely. She had the phone password protected. Luckily it wasn't an iPhone, not that that did us any good. She'd deleted the phone's history and files and reset it to factory specs before leaving it. And to confuse things even further, her mom's credit card was used at a Phillips 66 in Platte City just north of the I-435 turn-off to Topeka. We expanded our search west based on the GPS history and the credit card usage. You can imagine how . . . *surprised* we were to find out she was here instead."

I tried to keep from laughing. I imagined *pissed* was more likely than *surprised*. This was one very clever girl. But where is she now?

"You mentioned that the father was a colleague. Was he one of your deputies?"

"No. Terry and I were in the same Nebraska Guard unit and served in Afghanistan together before I became sheriff. He was wounded, sent home and quit the Guard while I finished out my tour. We're also old friends. Met in high school. When I got back from 'Stan I went back to my job as deputy. Sheriff Baynard decided to retire and I ran to replace him. I was elected sheriff last year. So, what do you say? Can I hire you to find Tessa Ryker?"

"Will Blank County be paying us?"

"No, ma'am. No way the county board would approve it and it can't come out of my department budget. I'm paying the freight on this."

"Okay, then. We can try to find her if she's here or try to get a lead on where she may have gone but make no promises. Our rate is $150 an hour with an up front $1,500 retainer. That covers ten hours and normal expenses. That may not sound like a lot of time, but we're good at what we do. We should have something by tomorrow but not necessarily what you want. Beyond that, that's up to you."

Two

Tessa escaped the carnage at her home. Drove south away from Hartfield, away from the sheriff that murdered her father, her mother, her sister. Destroyed her family. She didn't know why it happened, didn't know where she was going — just knew she needed to get as far away as quickly as possible.

She pulled out her phone when it dinged. She had a text message from Brian wanting to know why she wasn't at school. Said he'd have cut class with her if he'd known. He added a disappointed emoji. Tessa smiled. Maybe he did really care for her as hard as that was to imagine. He was a senior after all and she was just a freshman.

Allie and Sam thought he was playing her. He'd been hinting a lot about sex. She loved him, she thought, and wanted to please him, but she wasn't ready for that. That was why she had been at the creek. Trying to think things out, decide what to do, when she heard those shots.

Tessa felt the truck shake as it drifted onto the shoulder of the road. She pulled back into her lane and focused on driving. She glanced at the phone. Should she text Brian back? Tell him about the sheriff killing her family? Ask him what —

She suddenly realized the sheriff could track her phone's GPS. Could use that to find her. She turned the phone off and kept driving south.

She stopped at a welcome center to use the restroom, buy snacks and a drink, and study the huge display map. As she was deciding where to go an older, red F-150 with Texas plates parked beside her truck. A man in his mid-twenties got out, stretched and headed for the restrooms. That gave her an idea.

Tessa went to her truck, got out her phone and turned it on. She deleted the photos she'd taken and logged out of her cloud account. She logged out of her Facebook, Snapchat, Twitter, Instagram and email accounts then deleted the accounts from the phone. She deleted history, encrypted the phone and did a factory reset. Leaving the phone turned on, she stuck it behind the red truck's toolbox. Let the sheriff track that! She got in her truck and pulled out as the man was returning.

When the gas gauge read half full, she stopped and filled up using her mom's credit card at the pump. Then she remembered the cop shows where they traced credit card usage. She tossed the card in a trashcan and got back on the highway. A few miles down the road she had to decide whether to go southwest toward Topeka or southeast toward Kansas City. Her phone was headed for Texas she was pretty sure. Tessa chose east.

She passed Kansas City following the interstate east several more hours with no real plan. Where could she go? Where could she hide? Who would help her? Once the sheriff knew she was gone how could he find her? Do a whatchamacallit on the truck? Get other states' police involved? How long before that happened? She had to get rid of it. The glow from the city in the distance drew her like a moth to a flame.

Tessa drove into the city searching for the bus station. Finding it, she parked several blocks away, put her long hair up and donned a pair of her dad's readers from the glove box. She locked the truck. She'd come back for her stuff once she bought a ticket and knew when the bus left. She walked to the station. She decided she'd try to get to Aunt Beckie's in Seattle. Should have headed that way in the first place. Aunt Beckie would hide her, surely. Maybe get her into Canada where no one would find her.

Tessa walked quickly from the station angry and scared. The ticket lady wanted ID she didn't have. Asked if she were a runaway. Wanted to connect her with the National Runaway Switchboard to get her a free ticket home. Home! Right! That's the last place she wanted to be. And the last thing she wanted was authorities knowing where she was.

She got back in the truck and drove aimlessly through the strange city where she knew no one. She had to dump the truck soon, she knew, but was reluctant to leave it. It was her dad's. A last link she hated to sever. Tired, she parked on a deserted street beside a dilapidated, boarded-up movie theater. She closed her eyes for a moment. A siren woke her. An EMS truck with lights flashing crossed a block ahead.

Tessa turned the key on to look at the clock: 2:37. She'd fallen asleep. She looked around. There were no cars on the street, no one walking. Her eye caught an old movie poster displayed on the side of the building. It was half torn, but the announcement above it read, "Now Playing *Boys Don't Cry.*" She remembered seeing the movie on cable with her mother and crying at the time. Tears slid down her cheeks as she remembered her mom.

They'd made popcorn that night and had a bag of chocolate kisses. Mom made hot cocoa. It was just the two of them. Trina was asleep; Dad was at the VA hospital in Omaha overnight because of complications with his recovery. Tessa had been worried, but Mom said it was just a routine exam and he'd be back home soon. It had been pleasant curled with her mom on the couch watching the movie. Tessa wiped the tears from her cheeks. I miss you Mom.

She stared at the poster. Could I pass for a boy? I'm tall. In pretty good shape from sports and farm work. My breasts are small. Tape them like Brandon did in the film?

Tessa started the truck and went looking for a Walmart. She found an all-night Walgreens first. She went in. Didn't see any other customers. Found a combo haircutting kit, a large hand mirror, black hair color and two 6-inch wide elastic bandages. She grabbed a bag of Hershey's Kisses on her way to the counter.

The woman at the register looked nineteen or twenty and was a couple of inches shorter than Tessa. Her magenta hair was a blunt bowl cut with the sides and back shaved. Her left eyebrow was pierced and there were three gold rings piercing her right ear. She looked at the items Tessa placed on the counter and smiled.

"Going for a new look or lifestyle?"

Tessa blushed then looked anxious. She didn't say anything.

"Sorry. Didn't mean to embarrass you." The woman rang up the items. "That'll be $56.87."

Tessa pulled out cash and sorted it as the woman bagged her items. The woman gave her a worried look.

"Are you okay? You in some kind of trouble?"

Tessa shakily put two twenties, three fives and two ones on the counter but said nothing. Put the rest of the cash back in her pocket. The woman looked toward the door then back at her.

"Are you hiding? Is someone after you? I can help if you need it."

Tessa looked anxiously at the exit then back at the woman's concerned blue eyes.

"How?" she whispered.

"By finding you a safe place. My name's Paula. Are you in immediate danger?"

Tessa shook her head. "Not yet, but . . ." Tears ran down her face as the enormity of her situation engulfed her.

Paula came from behind the counter and took Tessa in her arms. She watched the entrance as she let the terrified girl bury her face against her and cry. Spoke softly to her.

"It's okay. It'll be okay. Don't worry. Do you have somewhere to go?"

"N-No."

"No one who can help you?"

"No."

"That's all right. I can help you. I'll make you safe."

Tessa raised her face from Paula's shoulder. "Why would you help me?"

"Anonymity. It's a group I belong to. It's what we do."

Paula went back to the register, canceled the sale and took the bag, cash and Tessa to the office.

"I'm here alone. No one comes in before six. That couch is pretty comfortable. You can sleep for a bit."

Tessa fell asleep right away and fortunately had no dreams. At 5:30, Paula woke her and sent her to a diner three blocks south next to a convenience store on the corner.

"I'm off at seven." Paula gave her a red baseball cap. "This'll help hide your face. Wait for me there and I'll meet you."

The convenience store was closed, as was the library across the street. The neon *OPEN* sign at Belle's Diner was lit, and Tessa could see through the large windows only a few people at the counter. When she walked in the smell of bacon frying hit her and made her realize she hadn't really eaten since breakfast the day before. There was a row of booths along the front windows and the counter ran nearly back to an old-fashioned jukebox and the restrooms. The booths were empty. She sat in the last one with her back to the rest of the restaurant. She could see the whole room and everyone reflected in the end window. The lone waitress brought her a menu and she ordered bacon, eggs, a strawberry waffle and coffee.

At 7:06, when Paula joined her, the place was full. As she sat down, Paula smiled when she saw that Tessa was wearing black-framed glasses as well as the cap. They made the girl look older.

"You okay?"

Tessa nodded.

Paula ordered orange juice, coffee and a toasted bagel with cream cheese. Tessa had a second waffle with strawberries and whipped cream.

As they ate, Paula looked up. The next booth was empty and hadn't been bused and no one was at this end of the counter. She leaned toward Tessa, talking low.

"Does who's after you know you're here?"

Tessa shook her head and swallowed a big bite.

"I don't think so. Not yet, anyway. But I'm sure the cops will be looking for the truck I'm driving."

"Why?"

Tessa wasn't sure why she should trust this woman, but she did. She gave few details but told Paula how she found her family after seeing the sheriff come out of their house and her running off.

"You think he did it?"

"Who else could have? He was there. I saw him. He came out right after I heard the shots. And that gun in my dad's hand? We don't have any guns. The sheriff must have left it there. That's why I'm afraid. Who's going to believe me over him? He's the sheriff. He'll know as soon I go to the cops. Might have everyone looking for me already. I thought disguising myself as a guy might keep him from finding me."

Paula sat back, sipped her coffee and stared at Tessa. She put the cup down. "Let's get out of here."

They put Tessa's things in Paula's car and left the unlocked truck near the bus station with the key in it. They went to Walmart and bought men's clothes, Reebok cross trainers and a large, black, travel duffel then went to Paula's apartment.

"I've only got one bedroom but that futon folds down. I'll get you a pillow, sheets and blanket. You're safe here. You need more sleep and I definitely do so we'll talk later. I'll put a fresh towel and washcloth in the bathroom if you want to shower."

They talked later over a lunch of grilled cheese sandwiches and packaged ramen improved with miso, scallions and leftover chicken.

"I skipped school yesterday because of my boyfriend. I needed time to think. He's older—a senior—and wants sex already. I love him, I think. Love being with him, anyway, but I'm . . . I'm not ready for that. I mean, God, I'm only fourteen."

Paula sat back. "Fourteen? I was thinking seventeen, maybe sixteen. But fourteen? You're so tall."

Tessa shrugged. "Yeah. Always tallest in my class. Anyway, that's why I was at the creek when I heard the shots. That was strange 'cause we don't own any guns. Dad got rid of all of them after he came back from Afghanistan. He'd been wounded over there. He doesn't—" Tessa stopped and tried to keep from crying. "He *didn't* talk about what happened or what he did there. I was trying to understand why someone was shooting when I came out of the woods and saw the sheriff leave our house and drive away. Then I found . . . Sorry. I don't want to talk about that. It's . . ."

Paula reached over and took her hand. "I understand."

They sat quietly like that for several minutes.

"You said you could help me. How?"

"First off, I'll cut your hair and you can try on your new clothes. Let's see how you look as a guy. Then we'll see about getting you a new identity."

"You can do that?"

Paula nodded. "Through Anonymity, I can."

"You mentioned them. Who are they?"

"We're an underground domestic violence and abuse organization. Very private but well organized. We bend the rules where others can't."

"Like making fake IDs?"

"Like that and more. We can even move you almost anywhere too. If you want."

"Really?"

"Really."

"God. That must cost a lot." Tessa wondered if she should tell her about the bag of money. "I don't—"

"We don't charge," Paula interrupted. "I can't speak for everyone in Anonymity, but most of us have been where you are now. We understand like others can't. We help because someone once helped us. I wasn't always Paula Fowler nor am I originally from here. Trust me. We'll do whatever it takes to make you safe. Give you a whole new life if you want."

"Let me think about it. I'm too confused right now."

"Sure. That's understandable. No need to rush. It may take some time to get the right ID. Meanwhile, you can stay with me. If anyone asks, you're my cousin visiting for a few weeks. What first name do you want to use?"

Tessa thought of her father, tried to forget how she last saw him. "Terry."

"All right, Terry. Let's get you sheared."

He played with his food at dinner, hardly eating. Kept glancing at the phone. The damn phone that never rang. His wife asked if he were all right and he snapped at her. He kept his head down but looked at his wife out of the corner of his eye. How was she going to react when she heard her friend Caroline was dead? Murdered. His kids looked concerned by his actions. He apologized, said it'd been a hectic day, but he still didn't feel like eating. Couldn't keep the picture of the little girl in the pantry closet out of his head.

He had no idea what they watched on television after dinner. He kept reliving what happened at the farmhouse. Kept wishing for the phone to ring. Why hasn't Tessa Ryker reported it yet? Where is she? Why was the little girl home? Damn. Damn.

Later he tossed and turned through the night waking at every noise and reaching for the phone that didn't ring. The little girl haunting him.

He returned to the office early, his head pounding, his stomach churning and sour from too much coffee without breakfast, too many aspirin and antacid tablets. He grabbed the overnight reports and went to his desk. Nothing! Where the fuck was that girl? Why haven't the killings been reported?

There was an auto accident five miles west of town on State Road 91 at 9:23 that took most of the morning tying up three deputies and a detective. Aside from that, everything was quiet.

Near noon the dispatcher buzzed him.

"Sir, the high school's reporting a truancy and asked if we'd do a drive-by."

"Who is it, Andy?"

"Ninth grader name of Tessa Ryker.

"Did you say Ryker? What's the story?"

"Yes, sir. School says she didn't come to class today and that she was truant yesterday too. Said they talked to the mother yesterday but haven't been able to reach either parent this morning. Family's farm is south off 133. Should we send someone out there?"

Fuck! Why wasn't she in school yesterday? Where was she? Was she at the farm? Could she have seen me there? Shit! Does she know I —

"Sir?"

"What?"

"Should we send someone?"

"Yes. Yes. Definitely. See who's closest. Keep me informed."

Three

With Sheriff Donahue's $1,500 check and a signed contract filed away, we spent another hour talking with him and looking through that thick file folder he'd brought. As I rarely see police files except when they're provided through discovery to defense counsel I've worked for, this file contained a lot more information than we needed for locating Tessa Ryker.

A Deputy Sharon Olson had discovered the victims Oct. 9 at 12:28 p.m. Megan Donahue, the Uriah Blank High School secretary (and the Sheriff's cousin), had asked that someone go to the Ryker farm as Tessa Ryker was not in school for the second day in a row and the parents could not be reached. The secretary had spoken with Mrs. Ryker Oct. 8 at 11:22 a.m. about Tessa's original truancy but got no answer this time. The school secretary's conversation with Mrs. Ryker helped establish time of death, which the county medical examiner estimated occurred between noon and 2:00 p.m., Oct. 8.

When Deputy Olson arrived at the home, the front door was open and she found Ronald Terrence Ryker (45) on the living room floor dead from a gunshot to the head. Forensic pathology established it was a contact wound from beneath the chin aimed upward sending the bullet through the brain and removing part of the top of the skull resulting in immediate death. GSR (gunshot residue) was found on the victim's hands as well as beneath the chin and on the front of the victim's shirt.

The second victim, Caroline Alice Ryker (40), was found in the central hallway leading from the living room. She had been shot twice. Once in the upper back by the left shoulder blade and once at the base of the skull. The bullet from the head wound exited through the victim's left cheekbone just below the eye socket and had lodged in the hall wall. No GSR was found suggesting the victim was fleeing and not near her killer. Death was ruled immediate or within minutes. A third bullet was later recovered from the living room wall next to the hall entry supporting the theory that the victim was fleeing her killer when shot.

The third victim, Katrina April Ryker (8), was found on the floor of the kitchen pantry. She had been shot once in the head behind the left ear at close range from a downward angle suggesting she was hiding and that the killer stood in the doorway above her. Death was ruled immediate.

No other victims were found in the home or immediate area. The remaining daughter, Tessa Anne Ryker (14), was missing. Whereabouts unknown. Tessa's friends and acquaintances were questioned. All were shocked, had no idea where she might be and hadn't heard from her.

Bullets and shell casings recovered were 9x19mm Parabellum. No murder weapon was recovered. No other weapon or ammunition was found in the home.

Missing from the home was Tessa's parka, several clothes, a pink sports bag and her laptop computer; Caroline Ryker's driver license and a credit card (used later Oct. 8 to buy fuel); an unknown amount of cash; and a 2010, white, Ford F-150 SuperCrew, Nebraska License # QIZ 994.

An APB for all Nebraska and neighboring states was issued Oct. 9 at 6:47 p.m. for the pickup truck and for Tessa Anne Ryker (DOB: 12/28/2004; SEX: F; HGT: 5'-09"; WGT: 129 lb; EYES: Brown; HAIR: Brown). APB updated Oct. 10 to include Idaho, Oregon and Washington. APB updated Oct. 14

to include Oklahoma, Texas, New Mexico, Arizona and California. APB on truck rescinded Oct. 20. APB on Tessa Ryker expanded to Illinois, Kentucky, Tennessee and Arkansas.

Barb turned pale looking at the crime scene photos. I avoided them and concentrated on those of Tessa Ryker.

"She's quite tall for a fourteen-year-old. Could easily be mistaken for being older. With the right make-up and clothes, possibly eighteen or nineteen."

Sheriff Donahue nodded. "She's athletic too. Plays basketball, field hockey and baseball as well as working at the farm."

"A good student?"

"Average. Cs in most classes. I'm told that's because she doesn't study, rushes her homework assignments last minute and cuts classes. Teachers say she's capable of being an A student."

"So what do you think happened at the house?"

"As I said before, there are conflicting opinions. At first, it looked like murder/suicide. Ryker killing his wife and daughter then himself. His wound and the GSR on his hands support that. Problem is the weapon is gone. Was the killer someone else? Can't understand why Tessa would take the weapon and run away if she only came home and found them dead instead of calling nine-one-one."

"That does seem strange."

"The second possibility was that an unknown person and Tessa's father fought over the gun, Ryker was killed and then the others killed. Why is a mystery, and, for whatever reason, Tessa was kidnapped and taken away in the stolen truck instead of being killed also."

"But that doesn't jibe with Tessa hiding her phone in that other truck. That looks more like she's avoiding being found."

"Exactly. Which brings us to the theory my chief deputy and the county prosecutor believe. That Tessa fought with and killed her father—possibly accidentally—then killed her mother and sister to hide the fact and ran away to escape prosecution. Her biggest mistake was not leaving the gun with her father. That would have supported the murder/suicide theory. Her phone's GPS history says she was in the area at the time of the killings. And the dogs we had out looking for her traced her scent to a swimming hole down by the creek behind the farm. We searched the creek for the murder weapon but didn't find it. So I don't know what to believe and won't know until Tessa is found and questioned."

"Maybe," Barb said. We looked at her. "Maybe she . . ."

Barb hesitated, her eyes flashing back and forth between us before she continued.

"What . . . what I mean is, maybe when she found them, she didn't want to believe her father could do such a thing. Girls love their fathers after all. So she took the gun and ran away so he couldn't be blamed. Just a thought."

For some reason I wasn't sure that was all Barb meant to say but I understood her reasoning.

"That's something we'll have to ask when we find her." I turned back to the sheriff. "Assuming Ryker killed his family, why did he do it? Marital problems? Debts? What?"

"Nothing we could find. Everyone says the marriage was solid. No affairs or anything like that. Bills piled up while Terry was in 'Stan, but the farm's doing well now. No bills or debts in arrears. Some think it was PTSD-related. We saw some nasty stuff over there and then Terry was wounded with a long recovery. He was still seeing doctors at the VA hospital in Omaha before his death, but we haven't been able to find out exactly why. He quit the Guard when he came home. And although he and I've visited and talked a lot since then, we don't—didn't—discuss how either of us were affected by our tour. So he's never really opened up to me."

"Do you think Tessa has the murder weapon?"

"Possibly, if the killer isn't someone else. GSR on Ryker's hands makes it plausible he had the gun. I don't want to believe it. That's not the Terry I knew. The fact is the gun's gone. Tessa's gone. Have to consider she has it."

"Maybe I'm charging you too little for finding her. An armed and scared teenager is not my cup of tea. The bullets were nine millimeter. What do you think the weapon is?"

"There are a lot to choose from but probably a Beretta 92FS. Terry trained with the M9 version in the Guard and carried one in Afghanistan. The bullets used in the killings were consistent with standard NATO rounds. Don't know if he owned a Beretta or not, but according to Bill Taggart at Taggart's Targets, Terry didn't buy one from him. Fact is, Terry sold all his guns to Taggart when he came home from Afghanistan. The only handgun was an old .22 Smith & Wesson revolver. Right now we don't know exactly what the murder weapon is or where it came from."

"Does Tessa have a boyfriend? Maybe they were together and the boy had the gun."

"Considered that. Boy's name is Brian Miller. He's seventeen. A senior. Basically a good kid from a good family. Never in any serious trouble. Cuts classes occasionally, but he was definitely in school the day of the murders. Family owns shotguns and rifles like most everybody but no handguns. Said he texted her right after school that day. She didn't answer and he hasn't heard from her. We tapped his cell as well as those of her two closest friends, Allison Murphy and Samantha Evans. They've all texted her several times but got no answer. But that's because her phone's in custody. And she hasn't tried to call or text any of them so far."

"Does she use Facebook or email?"

"Both, but there's been no activity there. Same with her Twitter account. We got warrants to access those. Boyfriend and friends' accounts too so we can see if she gets in contact some other way."

"Snapchat is the hottest among teens," Barb said, "followed by Instagram. Have you checked those? Facebook and Twitter have really fallen off. Less than ten percent of teens use it now."

Donahue made a note in his pad. "I'll mention it to Detective Anderson though I'm sure she's probably already thought of it. She and Joe Kern are my lead investigators on this."

I was looking at the bus station surveillance photos of Tessa Ryker as they spoke. The photos were grainy but it was definitely Tessa. The glasses and bun made her look older but the pink lining showing on her puffy parka countered that. Mostly what came through was she looked scared.

Scared of *what* was the big question. Was she running from the killer? Had she seen him or her? If so, why not call the police or go to them? Or contact them when she got far enough away to feel safe? Had she killed her family like some thought? Why? Because she got caught cutting school? Was there an argument? Was she pregnant and they fought over it? Where did the gun come from? Who brought it? Why wasn't it there if Ryker killed his family? I looked at the sheriff.

"Any chance the girl's pregnant and she fought with her father about it?"

"Asked Brian that same question. He got real red and tried evading but finally admitted that he'd been trying to get her to have sex but they hadn't yet."

"Are her and her friends' social media accounts in this file?" Barb asked.

"Yes, but there's been no activity or contact as I said."

Barb nodded. "We'll check them anyway. Just in case. Going two weeks without being connected isn't easy. She's scared and alone. I'm surprised she hasn't reached out already."

"Debra—that's Detective Anderson—thinks so too. Thinks we're missing something. She keeps going through all the postings trying to find something. Wants more warrants for other kids' accounts. Judge hasn't agreed to it yet."

I passed the surveillance photos to Barb. She laughed.

"What?"

"The glasses. Bet they're readers from a dollar store. Plus ones, maybe. Something low that doesn't bother her vision much but changes her look. She's scared but smart."

I nodded. "Sheriff, anything else we need to know that's not in this file?"

"Think that's it. There are contact numbers for my office, my investigators and Chief Deputy Harold Wagner. Harry's in charge till I get back. My personal cell is in there too. I'll let them all know I've hired you so you can share info and vice versa."

"Thanks. We'll be in touch. You headed back right away?"

"No. The funerals aren't till Monday. I'll be back for those. Your Channel 3 wants to interview me this afternoon. After that, thought I'd wander and do some looking on my own till you get back to me."

"You really think she's still here?"

He nodded. "Enough that I'm willing to spend money on you. Just my gut feeling, though. Can't explain it. Hate what happened. They were a wonderful family and good friends. I need to find her. It ain't right. I need to fix it."

"Understand. Where you staying?"

"Sunrise Motel out on Cutter Avenue."

"Some good restaurants out that way. If you like Tex-Mex, try Amigos. The food's great. They're further west on Cutter at 73rd Street. We'll have an update for you sometime tomorrow."

Sheriff Donahue left and Barbara and I sat back down.

"What do you think?"

Barb sighed. "I'm not sure. Tessa's scared. That's obvious. But is she running from the killer or the cops?"

"That's the problem. She's not going to trust anyone looking for her. Think she'll be in the usual places?"

"No way to know, but we have to check. I mean, she's alone as best we know; can't have a whole lot of money. I mean, how much cash did her parents keep at home? A few hundred bucks for odds and ends and emergencies, at best. Right?"

"That's my thinking. It's been two weeks. If she's here, where's she staying? How much money is left? What have you got today?"

Barb picked up her iPad and scrolled through it.

"The only thing that can't wait until tomorrow is my interview with Cory Gallagher. He's a potential witness in the Haynes case. I finally found him and we're meeting at three."

"I've got a one o'clock downtown with Warren Daniels. It's a final report on his missing wife. Doubt he's going to be happy that she's across the river living with his cousin. Or that the cousin's been embezzling company funds to support his and Mrs. Daniels' love nest. We've also got a backlog of background checks to finish. When's Jen coming in again?"

"Luckily today. Noon or one, I think. Said she could give us all day Friday."

"Okay. She can work on the background checks."

"I'd rather have her work on Tessa's friends if that's all right. I can't believe Tessa hasn't reached out to someone back home. I think the sheriff's people missed it. Face it, finagling the Internet is Jen's favorite pastime."

"All right. We'll split the backgrounds. Can't leave them hanging. But, first, let's make some calls on Tessa."

I stopped at the door to my private office and turned back.

"Barb?"

"Yes?"

"When we were talking to Sheriff Donahue you suggested Tessa took the gun to keep her father from being blamed."

"That's right. Why?"

"You hesitated. Was there something else you thought of? Something you didn't want to share with the sheriff?"

"It was just a crazy notion."

"What was it?"

"What if Tessa saw the killer and recognized him. You know, someone important in the community whose word would be believed over hers. Especially if the gun was found with her dad and the killings ruled a murder/suicide. Crazy, huh?"

"Not crazy at all. Might explain why she hasn't gone to the police yet. She must be scared. Doesn't know who to trust. She's only fourteen. What does she do? As far as we know, she doesn't know anyone here. So, where does she go? Where would you go?"

"PJs. I was a runaway too, remember?"

"I remember. If anyone mentioned PJs to her, that'd be my first choice too. Let's hit the phones."

I went to my old teacher's desk that has served me well since opening my agency. I still keep my private office looking a lot like the high school classroom it originally was. The reception area and Barb's and Jen's alcoves may be new and modern, but I love the old blackboard and the smell of chalk, the two rows of student tables I still use occasionally for cases and the huge windows that afford wonderful sky views especially at sunset.

I booted my laptop and opened my contact list. Over the years my list of reliable contacts has grown from PJs runaway refuge, Ariana Feldman, Interfaith Harvest and the YW and YMCA, to include The Lillith Society, the Hare Krishnas, Our Lady of Hope, Youth in Need, Youth Emergency Services, Baptist Outreach, Intervention, Cry For Help, Paying It Forward, Safe House, Las Doñas, Diversity, Karen's Place, The Sanctuary, Good Samaritans, Haven Hostel, Home Away, and the River Rats a loose community of homeless camps along the river.

PJs Johnson's two-story home has been a quasi-legal refuge for runaways and displaced youth for decades. It's one of those places you naturally gravitate to, feel comfortable and safe in. She's a big-hearted, big-framed woman with beautiful mahogany skin tones. She just turned 80, but is still active, always ready to give you a hug or a lecture as needed.

I'd always thought she was called PJs because of her penchant for wearing nothing but pajamas. She says they're the most comfortable clothing there is. She wears all styles, all colors, all kinds of material. A regular fashion queen of pajamas.

The truth is—as I discovered four years ago—she's been PJs all her life. She was named Paula Jasmine after her uncle, Paul Jasper Monroe. Born on his birthday. His family and friends called him PJ and everyone started calling her *PJ's girl*, later shortened to PJs.

PJ Monroe was a decorated veteran of World War II but that didn't stop him being lynched in 1947 at Hangman's Oak in Gardner Park. Stories at the time said he was an uppity black—though the term used wasn't *black*—because he demanded respect for his military service while others—mostly whites—got deferments and prospered at home. Or it may have happened because he was gay or because many women of every color enjoyed his company. Whatever the reason, no one was arrested despite rumors of who did it.

I got involved in the story when four years ago on the anniversary of Monroe's lynching George Armstrong Cutter was found hanging at Hangman's Oak. Cutter was one of many originally suspected of killing Monroe but never charged. The Cutter family was renowned in the area. George's father died a hero in World War II. The local American Legion chapter is named after him, while Cutter Avenue is named for an honored ancestor.

The police thought Cutter's death was a vengeance crime for that long ago lynching and were questioning PJs' relatives and threatening arrests. PJs hired me to find the truth. The truth turned out that George Cutter was dying of cancer and hanged himself. He chose suicide as a better alternative to a lingering death hooked up to machines and zonked on medications. He also regretted his role in killing Monroe saying so in a statement I found along with a photograph showing the lynching and the six men involved.

PJs' eldest daughter, Ruth, answered the phone. She looks a lot like her mother and is filled with the same big-hearted love for anyone who needs it.

"Hey, Rachel. You and the girls get lost? Haven't seen you, Jennifer or Barbara in a dog's age."

"Sorry for being absent. It has been awhile. You still have Thursday spaghetti night?"

"Do chickens lay eggs? Course we do."

"Plan on us being there tomorrow then. I'll tell Barb and Jen."

"Good. Be great to see you all. And bring that pretty wife of yours too. Our sauce is vegan and we have vegan meatballs available. More 'n more of the youngsters coming here are vegetarian."

"I'll tell Wendy, thanks."

"I know you're not calling just to chat. What do you need? Looking for anyone in particular?"

"Have you seen the news about the family murdered in Nebraska and the missing daughter?"

"We have, and before you ask, no, she hasn't been here. Sergeant Wainwright from Missing Persons called and asked us yesterday. We asked everyone here if they've come across her, but no one has. Are you looking too?"

"Yes. We've been hired by a concerned family friend."

"We'll keep asking but I think she's long gone. If she were still in the city, she'd have found us afore now."

"My thoughts too. Thanks, Ruth. Give my best to PJs."

None of my other calls produced immediate results and Barb was still on the phone when it was time for me to leave. At least the word was getting out. Waiting for the feedback is the real bitch.

Jen hadn't arrived. I left it for Barb to fill her in on what we needed her to do. Though two years younger, Jennifer Hackett was Barb's closest friend when I first met them at PJs. Jen helped me rescue Barbara from the pedophile. Later she lived with a foster family and took their last name when they adopted her. She graduated from Cramer College and works as a software designer for McManus Grimes Technologies south of town. She has no desire to be a full-time investigator. Which is good because there's no way I could match the money she makes at MGT. I'm just glad she enjoys helping us find runaways when it involves computer research.

Four

Tessa ran her hand over her bare neck while looking at herself in the bathroom mirror. It was the fifth time she'd done it. Her hair had never been that short. She was glad Paula talked her out of dying her hair. It wasn't necessary and would have stood out and looked odd.

She wore a loose, dark blue polo over a pair of straight leg Levis and, with her breasts tightly strapped, she had to admit Paula was right. She no longer looked like a girl. She felt safer. Maybe not safe, but safer.

She wondered what kind of ID Anonymity would make for her. Paula hadn't said but had taken her picture against a plain white background earlier. Tessa looked at her mirror image and smiled.

"Hey, Terry." She stopped, thought for a moment, tried to lower her voice to be more like Brian's. "Hey. What's a good-lookin' guy like you doin' in a place like this?"

She repeated the phrase and several others, practicing keeping her voice lower. It worked best when she slowed her speech slightly. When she was satisfied, she smiled again at her reflection adding a wink then sighed thinking of her boyfriend. If Brian hadn't bugged her about having sex, she wouldn't have cut school. Wouldn't have seen Sheriff Donahue. Wouldn't have found her family until . . . Tears welled in her eyes. She turned from the mirror brushing them away.

She went to the living room and sat on the futon. She didn't turn on the television. They'd watched the 10 o'clock news before Paula left for work and there was already coverage of her family's murders. There was a multi-state alert looking for her, her dad's truck and her presumed kidnapper.

Tessa felt both sick and angry. Sick that her family tragedy was being paraded across the country. Angry that Sheriff Donahue had the nerve to be interviewed and falsely convey the impression that he was concerned for Tessa's well being and wished her safe return. She knew what he really wanted: her dead just like her parents and sister. Well that wasn't going to happen. If anyone were going to die, it would be him, not her.

Tessa went to the coat closet and took the towel-wrapped gun from her bag. She hadn't told Paula about having the gun or about the Army duffel half-stuffed with cash. She was afraid. Afraid Paula would disapprove of her, of her father, of what her father may have done to have a hidden cache of money.

She'd never held a handgun. All she knew about them was what she'd seen in movies or television shows. The only gun she'd ever used or fired was the single-shot .410 her father gave her when she turned nine, and then only when Dad took her hunting for pheasant, doves or rabbits.

She remembered early mornings sitting with him at the edge of a field waiting for the first flurry of wings as a covey swept in. Those were special times. Just the two of them together, the sun edging over the horizon, the clear sky brightening from pre-dawn gray to blue. That was before he went to Afghanistan, before he came home wounded, changed. That was the last she'd seen of the .410. Although it was hers, it was sold with the rest of their guns.

She turned the gun from side to side. It was clearly stamped *U.S. 9mm M9-P.BERETTA-65490*. The hammer was pulled back just as it had been when she took it from her father's hand. Was it loaded?

This had killed her family. Bile rose in her throat. She laid the gun carefully on the coffee table not sure what to do. Not sure if she wanted to touch it again. She calmed herself. Stared at it for several minutes.

Can I prove the sheriff used this? How? She got her laptop and looked for an open Wi-Fi network. Paula hadn't said which was hers or what her password was. She got lucky, found one, went online, read various articles and watched YouTube videos.

Nervously, Tessa put the gun's safety on then went and got a plastic sandwich bag from the kitchen. Following the instructions she'd seen on YouTube, she released the clip into the bag. One forensic article she read mentioned fingerprints on clips and bullets. Maybe the sheriff's fingerprints would be on this. She swallowed when she saw the brass and copper bullet at the top of the clip. That could have killed me. She laid the clip aside. She pulled back the slide of the Beretta as she'd seen in several videos. She yelped and jumped as a bullet sprang across the room.

Shit! Tessa put the gun down. Afraid to touch it. Thought of how carelessly she had handled it at the house, in the truck. It could have gone off. Could have—Fuck me!

Calm again, Tessa found the bullet, picked it up with a tissue and put it in the sandwich bag with the clip. She carefully rewrapped the gun and clip in the towel, still slightly afraid of the unloaded weapon, and put them in her bag in the closet. She was too shaken to do anything else. She lay on the futon haunted by nightmares of her family and the silhouette of a man with a badge pointing a gun at her.

Paula saw the open laptop on the coffee table the next morning. She woke Tessa.

"Were you online last night?"

Tessa rubbed grit from her eyes. "Yeah. I wanted to check some things. Found an open network. You didn't tell me which was yours."

"Did you check your email or social accounts? Contact anyone?"

"No. I . . . I thought about doing that, but I . . . I was too tired and that stuff about my family on TV was too depressing. I just randomly surfed for a bit. Why?"

"You got rid of your phone because of GPS, right?"

"Yes."

"Well, your computer doesn't have GPS, but anything you do on the Internet leaves a trail too. The authorities will be looking at your accounts and your friends' accounts. If you log into your accounts or post to a friend, they can trace where and when you use your computer. The library. Starbucks. McDonalds. This building. Anywhere you connect to the Internet."

"I didn't know that. Sorry. What should I do?"

"Go dark. Don't access your accounts or contact anyone you know. There are ways to hide on the Internet, but, for now, it's safer to just lay low."

"Okay. I will." Tessa lowered her voice. "Say, ma'am, have you had breakfast yet? I'd be pleased to fix you something."

"That's great. Needs some work but definitely masculine." Paula curtsied. "Why thank you, sir. That's so kind of you." They both laughed. "Why don't we fix breakfast together?"

That night after Paula left for work, Tessa pulled out the cash-filled, Army duffel. She still hadn't told Paula about the money or the gun. Wasn't sure why. She trusted Paula. She'd done so much for her already. Was helping her stay safe. So why couldn't she tell her everything? She didn't know how to explain her reluctance any more than she knew why her family was murdered.

It had to be the money. What else could it be? She opened the duffel and began counting the cash. She went to the kitchen and found some rubber bands and a ball of twine. It took most of the night to count and bundle the money. $253,900 in tens, twenties and mostly hundreds. Wow. Dad? Where did you get all this? She turned the duffel inside out. There was nothing to indicate where it came from. How, Dad? Did the sheriff want this? I don't understand.

Tessa packed the money in her new sports duffel along with the gun putting some of her new clothes on top and put the duffel in the closet. She rolled up the Army duffel and put it in her old sports bag with her old clothes and shoes and put that in the closet too. She'd drop it at some thrift store in the next few days. She went to bed but was still awake thinking about the money when Paula came home. She pretended to be asleep.

The Ryker killings affected everyone in the department. Except for the few — like himself — who had been in Afghanistan or Iraq, none had experienced that kind of carnage. Particularly upsetting was the seemingly pointless murder of eight-year-old Katrina Ryker. The image of the little girl's body on the pantry floor preyed on everyone and goaded their efforts. Two-thirds of the department were at the Ryker farm searching for answers, searching for the missing daughter that everyone — except himself — thought must be dead also.

He was the first to arrive after Deputy Olson called in the report. She'd apologized for throwing up at the edge of the porch but he'd told her it was understandable given the circumstances. Then he'd purposely walked through the house with her without putting on gloves or shoe covers. He wasn't really worried that he'd left anything behind that would implicate him when he'd killed the family, but on the small chance something of his — DNA, a fingerprint, anything — did show up in the collection of evidence he'd have the excuse he accidentally left it in his initial search. As best he could tell, everything was as he'd left it except that the Beretta that should have been in Ryker's hand was missing. Did Tessa Ryker take it?

He stood on the porch of the Ryker farmhouse watching through the open doorway as several deputies collected evidence inside. The acrid smell of Olson's vomit was still noticeable, but was nothing compared to the stench of death in the house. Fortunately, he thought wryly, County Attorney Wade Vanderhorn hadn't added his own potentially upchucked lunch to Olson's.

As coroner by law under Nebraska's unique system, Vanderhorn — pale and clearly uncomfortable — had made a quick determination that the deaths were suspicious giving the sheriff's office full charge of the investigation before making a hasty retreat. After dozens of pictures were taken, the bodies were transported to the Douglas County Health Center in Omaha for autopsy to everyone's immediate relief.

He turned from the doorway and stepped to the edge of the porch placing his hand on a column. He looked out across the stubbled farm field where Deputy Dawson with his German shepherd Titan tracked a scent. Two other deputies followed. They stopped at the edge of the woods on the other side. The dog spent a lot of time checking one spot before going deeper into the woods. One of the deputies laid down a marker and took pictures.

Was the girl standing out there yesterday? Watching? Had she heard the shots? Did she see me standing here? Could she recognize me from that far away? Where is she? The gun's gone. The Ryker's truck is gone. Did she take it? And where's my fucking money?

The massacre of the Nebraska farm family filled the news cycle for several days. Pictures of the farmhouse, the family and the missing daughter were in every newspaper and on every television screen. Speculation was rife. Sheriff Baxter Donahue, Brian Miller, friends, friends' parents and even non-acquaintances were interviewed several times. Hundreds of leads poured in to the Blank County Sheriff's Office as well as to the FBI who was interested because of the possible kidnapping and interstate flight.

Little new information was released. When it was no one associated Paula's visiting cousin Terry with the missing Tessa Ryker. Not even when they were looking at her photograph and she was standing right in front of them.

"Why would such a pretty girl do something like that?" the convenience store clerk asked her.

Tessa's photo was displayed on the overhead television as two newscasters babbled about her phone being found in El Paso, Texas, and the search for her being extended west. Tessa looked at the elderly woman and shrugged.

"No idea, ma'am." She was getting used to lowering her voice and sounding more masculine and older. She laid a Kit Kat bar on the counter.

"Bet it was drugs like they say. Or some satanic thing."

Tessa—I'm not Tessa anymore, I'm Terry—shrugged again.

"I guess that's possible, ma'am. I'd also like to buy one of those phones."

"Which one?"

"How 'bout that one?"

"I've got one just like it. I love it. This for you?"

"No, ma'am. It's for my grandpa. He keeps losing his. Lost the last one while fishing at the river."

"Well, he can't go wrong with this one. Do you want an extra minutes card too?"

"Yes, ma'am. That'd be nice. Thank you."

Tessa—I'm Terry—looked up at the two newscasters still babbling, shrugged and left with her—*his*—purchase.

Texas? What the hell is she doing in Texas? Why did it take so damn long to find that out, damn it? And where's my money? It wasn't found during the search, luckily, but I haven't found it yet either. Has she got it? Does she know where it is? I need to find her. Need to get to her before anyone else. Texas? Why Texas?

It was difficult seeing the pictures of her family and farm on television and listening to different theories. Tessa became anxious as the days passed. She knew she needed to hide yet she wanted to know what was really happening at home. What her friends were doing. What they thought.

Paula had warned her that her and her friends' accounts were being monitored and their phones probably tapped. Still, a week had passed and Tessa felt so alone, so disconnected.

While Paula slept during the mornings, Tessa took her laptop to the local library to use the free Wi-Fi. She searched every story she could find online to see if there was any new and real information but everything was mostly a rehash and speculation. She stayed away from her own accounts but started checking her friends' public stuff without logging in figuring that would be safe.

Brian, Allie and Sam had posted their TV interviews on Facebook. They and other friends also posted comments on Twitter defending Tessa's innocence and begging her to get in contact. She was tempted to log on. Wanted badly to tell them what really happened and to see what they were posting in their private sections. Paula's warnings and the threat of Sheriff Donahue finding her kept her hesitating. Then she was shocked by a tweet at *HildySpeaksTrue* only a day old.

Unbelievable! Say it's not true, Tess. Tommy's dad says, "Evidence proves Tessa Ryker killed her family!!!!"

What? Tessa gaped at the message. No way! Tommy Wagner's dad is wrong. Hildred Speaks should know better to believe anything Tommy says. He exaggerates everything. How could she even think I would —

Tessa hit the reply bubble but only got the sign in message: *When you join Twitter, you can reply to anyone.* Damn! She hit the *Log in* button and stopped. Damn! She took a deep breath to calm down and think. She *had* to reply. Couldn't let it go unchallenged. Could she create a new account? She didn't have an email account to link it to. Did she know anyone's log in? She took a deep breath, logged in and replied.

It's a lie. Didn't do it. Sheriff Donahue did —

She stopped. No, I can't say that yet. I don't have the proof. If I say it, Hildy will tell everyone she knows. He'll know I saw him. She deleted *Sheriff Donahue did* and hit *Tweet* before she changed her mind.

I *had* to do it. Despite Paula's warning. I *had* to. She guiltily glanced around, quickly shut down her laptop and left the library.

Five

My meeting with Warren Daniels didn't go well. He slowly shook his head while looking at the pictures and financial records and reading the details of my report. He looked bewildered.

"Steve's stealing from me?"

"For at least two years that we can verify. The affair with your wife started a year before that."

"*Stealing* from me."

He shook his head with disbelief staring into space. He let out a deep sigh and reached for the phone.

"Sheila, please ask Mr. Raines to come to my office. Thank you."

He put the phone back and looked at the report again. He opened a drawer and took out a checkbook.

"Thirty-eight hundred, right?"

"That's correct. Sorry things turned out this way for you."

"Not your fault. I wanted to know. Now I know."

He handed me the check and mumbled something to himself. There was a knock before the door opened. Steven Raines, chief financial officer for Daniels Industries, came in closing the door behind him.

He was surprised Daniels wasn't alone. He looked at me as if he should know me but couldn't place where. That's because I was dressed very differently and wearing a dark wig when I offered him and Mrs. Daniels at their love nest across the river an expensive—and free—vacuum cleaner to test and then returned later to interview them on how well they liked it.

"Ah, you wanted to see me, Warren?"

"Yeah." Daniels' voice was calm. "How long you been skimming company funds as well as fucking my wife?"

Raines went pale, glanced at me, ran fingers across his lips.

"I . . . I don't know what you're talking about."

"The hell you don't. Fucking Peggy's one thing. Stealing from my company is a whole different matter, you bastard."

Daniels pulled a snub nosed revolver from the open drawer and shot Raines before I could yell, "Don't do it!" Raines fell. I dove across the desk tackling Daniels as he stood to shoot Raines again. The gun went off again as we hit the floor.

Several hours later, I had no idea of Raines' condition. Hopefully he was still alive. Daniels was in custody and I was—again, hopefully—finishing my interview with Det. Sgt. Melissa Wellborne and Det. Ryan Cassidy.

"No, again, I did not know Daniels owned a gun or that he had it in his desk. I had no idea he intended any violent action toward either his wife or Mr. Raines."

"What *did* you expect him to do?" Cassidy asked.

"Something civilized. Like divorce his wife and have Raines arrested for embezzlement."

Cassidy shook his head. "Are you really that dumb?"

I controlled myself from making an obscene comeback or gesture. It would be wasted on him and wouldn't get me out of there any quicker. Wellborne continued thumbing through a thick folder looking amused. She looked up.

"You've been involved in quite a lot of *violent action* over the years, haven't you?"

"Your point being?"

"No point. Just an observation." She tapped the folder. "Is there anything else you'd like to add to your statement?"

"No."

"That does it then." She flipped a switch on the microphones. "We'll have your statement ready to sign shortly. Would you like something while you wait?"

"No, thank you."

They left me alone in the barren, interview room. I didn't bother looking up at the one-way mirror. Had no desire to look at myself and didn't care if someone were watching me or not. Didn't care how long they'd leave me sitting here either. I'd read Daniels wrong. It may have cost a man his life. I didn't need to sit alone in a box to know that would prey on me for a long, long time.

I took out my phone to check time and messages. It was just after five and no messages. How did Barb's interview go? Had Jen found any leads? Were there any callbacks on someone seeing Tessa Ryker? Should I—

The door opened and I slipped my phone back into my bag.

"We have to stop meeting like this. People might think we're an item."

Lt. Denise Brody smiled as she leaned against the wall. Her maternity clothes did little to hide the basketball she carried.

"Maybe, but I highly doubt anyone's going to accuse me of being the father. When's the baby due?"

"Doctor says November nineteenth, but tomorrow would be fine with me."

"This your third?"

Denise nodded. "Third and done. Told Geordie either he gets fixed or I do."

We both laughed then she nodded toward the door.

"Melissa thinks you're holding back. Anything to it?"

"No. I told her exactly what happened as well as gave a full summary of our investigation for Daniels."

"Really? A *full* summary?"

"*In toto.* My detailed report for Daniels got scooped up along with all the other evidence. Figure your detectives will eventually read it. Why bother leaving something out that could bite me in the ass later? A masochist I'm not."

Denise laughed. "Really? Who'd have thunk it? I think this being the fourth time you've been in here giving a statement since I've been in command has Melissa concerned. I don't even want to think about the number of times before that."

"Shit happens and I sometimes get caught holding the pooper scooper. Not my idea of fun, believe me. Any news on Raines?"

"No. Still in surgery. Is it true you used a tampon to plug the wound?"

"Two actually. Old battlefield expediency. Use what's handy. The EMTs arrived quickly, so it probably didn't matter. Has Daniels' wife been notified?

Denise nodded. "Melissa called her at Raines' place. Said she sounded really upset but wasn't sure if it was for the husband or the lover. We've got a bet as to whether she comes here for her husband or goes to her lover's hospital. Want in?"

"No, thanks. How about my statement?"

"I'm told soon." She smiled. "Probably sooner if you join me for coffee in my office instead of sitting in here. Come on."

On the way to her office, we picked up coffee from the lounge and I thanked her for sending me Sheriff Donahue.

"Aside from the truck being found and her being seen at the bus station, they haven't any new leads, nor do we. Thought you'd have a different perspective and know people and places we don't."

"I'm not so sure. We're overlapping already. Wainwright's been ahead of me on four of the people I called this morning."

"Howard's good. Glad he got the job when I left Missing Persons. But there are going to be people who'll talk to you before they do him."

"True. Maybe we'll catch something. Then again, maybe we won't. We've put the word out to all our contacts. Now it's wait and see. Are you directly involved in the search?"

"No, Howard is. To Donahue, Tessa Ryker is a person of interest in a murder investigation. To us, she's just another missing teen who needs to be found. An important one, I'll admit, but not my department or primary concern. We have enough murders and attempted murders of our own to keep us busy without looking for more work."

Denise was right about sooner. We were barely settled in her office gabbing about other teens we'd worked together to find when Det. Cassidy brought my statement. I read, initialed and signed it and was back at the office 30 minutes later.

Six

The Ryker family massacre was becoming old news. There had been no updates on television or in the papers for days. Other atrocities had taken its place as well as the latest scandals from the White House and Congress' impeachment inquiry.

Tessa sat at the small breakfast table looking down on neighboring Radford Park. Several young children were climbing and sliding in the play area, their mothers sitting and talking nearby. In the distance, joggers and walkers were using the trails. It was a sunny, pleasant, peaceful morning.

The children made Tessa think of Trina. Trina laughing as Tessa pushed her on the tree swing behind the house. Trina tagging along to the movies or to one of Tessa's sporting events. Exploring the creek together. Fishing. Catching frogs and crickets. Collecting bright colored leaves in the fall. Teaching Trina how to use a blade of grass caught between her thumbs to make a whistling sound.

Tessa bit her lip to keep from screaming as she pictured Trina's lifeless body in the pantry. The feel of her cooling hand. Her eyes watered as she thought of her sister, her mother, her father dead.

Tessa wiped her eyes and looked to see if Paula saw her crying, but Paula was busy at the stove fixing breakfast. Tessa couldn't believe how lucky she'd been to find Paula.

She picked up the new driver's license and identity Paula had given her when she sat down. It was her picture with short hair on a Colorado license. The picture Paula had taken of her nearly two weeks ago. Two weeks? Already? Tessa glanced at the calendar on the wall. Tuesday, October 22. She was surprised at how much time had passed while the loss of her family still burned inside her. She looked at the license again.

She was now *Terrence Mayhew Romer; 135C Balsam Ave, Boulder CO 80306; DOB: 04-03-2000; Sex: M; Ht: 5'9"; Wt: 126; Eyes: BRO; Voter: Y; Donor: Y; Under 21, Expires 04-03-2021.* The license looked real. Paula hadn't said where it came from; only that Anonymity provided it.

Tessa—I'm really Terry now—stared at her new ID. *Terrence Mayhew Romer.* She—I'm *he* now. *He.* Need to remember that. Believe it. Wonder who I am?

Terry—yes, Terry. I'm Terry, Terry, Terry—took the other items out of the envelope Paula had given her—*him.* Given *him.* A Social Security card, a birth certificate, Selective Service card, voter registration, library card and an apartment rent receipt. A new name. A new me. So hard to believe.

Paula laid the plates of scrambled eggs, bacon and toast on the table and sat down.

"If you're wondering, that license *is* real. So is everything else. There's a two-page summary of your new life in there too. In a nutshell, you were born Samuel Clarence Long, Jr. in Blue Hill, Maine. Your parents, Sam senior and Carrie Belle, died in an auto accident near Bowling Green, Kentucky, in January 2003. So did the real Sam junior by the way. All three are buried there. But because states don't coordinate their vital statistics with each other, that fact may never come up."

"So how did I become Terry Romer?"

"Here's where creative license comes in. The Romers adopted you in July 2003, changed your name and moved you to Santa Fe, New Mexico. That's an amended birth certificate recording the change. You were a rebellious youth, didn't get along with your parents or complete high school but got your G.E.D. You moved out on your own to Colorado as soon as you turned eighteen. You made your own application for a name change to your Social Security card then because your adoptive parents hadn't done so earlier."

"This is so unreal. How did Anonymity do this?"

"I don't know the details. I'm not even sure how they made me who I am. I'm just glad they did. I think Anonymity has people working in vital statistics offices and other official positions around the country. People who can insert information into the necessary databases."

"I can't thank you enough for helping me. I'll never be able to repay you — or them — for this."

"No thanks or payment, necessary. As I said before, this is what we do. You're one of us now. If you ever meet someone in a similar situation needing help, then help her or him. I'll give you numbers you can use to contact Anonymity. But only when someone else needs them. That's how we repay."

"Have you done this before?"

"Twice. Once here. Once where I lived before."

"What do you think I should do now?"

"Go to Colorado. Or anywhere you want. Make a new life for yourself. Study. Go to college. Become whoever you want to be. That address is real by the way. It's one of two studio apartments in a private home. It's waiting for you."

"That won't help me get Sheriff Donahue for killing my family."

"Tess, you're fourteen. What can you do?"

"I don't know, but I have to try. I've got to get him."

"Vengeance won't bring your family back. Let go. It'll eat you if you don't."

"I have to do it."

"You could get killed too, you know. Let it go."

"I can't."

That night Terry looked out the living room window at Radford Park. The park was empty. It was dark and the children were gone, home having dinner, doing homework, getting ready for bed. Paula was taking a shower. They planned to watch a movie before Paula went to work. They hadn't talked more about what he should do. He turned to the closet where the duffel with the money and M9 Beretta lay. He — yes, I'm *he* now — still hadn't told Paula about them. Should I? What would she say? She's been nothing but wonderful. Done nothing but help me. Why am I still afraid to tell her? Is it because of you, Sheriff? Is it because I'm afraid she'd take the gun away from me? Because if you aren't jailed for murdering my family, damn you, I'm going to kill you with it.

This is ridiculous. How is it possible for a 14-year-old to make fools of every law enforcement agency in the country? We've got half the West looking for her when she headed east instead. Finally, the truck's been found and she was seen. Twelve fucking days ago! At a Greyhound station for Christ's sake! And we're just finding this shit out now?

There's got to be another way to find her.

Seven

Barb turned from her computer.

"Where were you? Thought you'd be back long before me."

"Daniels shot Raines."

"What?"

Jennifer stuck her head out from behind her cubicle panel. Her eyes and mouth were large circles.

"You're joking, right?"

"No joke, ladies. We were discussing the report when he called Raines to the office and shot him while I sat there. Had no idea he had a gun or planned to use it. I got it away from him. Raines was still in surgery last I heard. Daniels is arrested and I spent the last hours being questioned."

I collapsed onto one of the visitor chairs and dropped my bag at my feet. They rushed over.

Jennifer pointed. "You tore your pants."

I glanced at the two-inch rip above the knee. There was also a trace of blood. Great. Another ruined outfit. I touched the area. It was tender but didn't really hurt.

"Must have happened when I tackled Daniels across his desk."

"Tackled? Are you all right?"

"Mostly. My ego's bruised and I'm still upset it happened. I didn't figure Daniels as being violent."

Barb sat beside me. "Have you called Wendy?"

"Yes. On my way here. Didn't want her to see it on the news first if my name gets mentioned. How'd your interview with Gallagher go?"

"Great. He'll be a good witness. He remembered the incident clearly and had no problem being recorded. I sent a copy of my report and the recording to Truman by messenger an hour ago."

"Good. Any progress on finding Tessa Ryker?"

Barb shook her head. "Only six call backs so far. All negative."

"It's a long shot if she's still here. How 'bout you, Jen?"

"I've got the list of accounts of Tessa and her friends the Sheriff gave you and looked at all of them. I added six other people based on who Tessa and her friends were following on Twitter. I'm downloading everyone's Tweets and replies now going back to the third and running a program that'll filter out every mention of Tessa and the killings."

"You've done all that already?"

Jen smiled. "The computers are doing it. I just gave the instructions. Makes that upgrade I convinced you to pay for worthwhile, doesn't it. I'm doing the same with their Facebook accounts as I make friends with them. So far Samantha Evans, Tommy Wagner, Allison Murphy and Christina Lopez have friended me. There's a lot of stuff on everyone's public pages but I need to be friends to get to the good stuff."

"I'm impressed."

"Don't be, yet. Snapchat and Instagram are harder nuts to crack. I need to access their main servers to get what we want. They claim to the public nothing is saved but that's not true. There's a program we're beta testing at MGT for the government I could use to hack in, but didn't think you'd approve."

"You're right. I don't approve. If we weren't working *with* the Law, I'd think about it though. Let's let Donahue's detectives—" I turned to Barb. "What are their names, again?"

"Anderson and Kern."

"Right. They can get court orders and warrants. Let them handle Snap whatever and that other one."

Barb and Jen both smiled at my lack of keeping up with social media.

"Wipe the smirks from your faces. This is why I keep you two around."

The office phone rang. Jen picked it up.

"Confidential Investigations. How may I help you? One moment, please."

Jen put the phone on hold. "It's Tanya Waverly from Channel 3."

I took the phone. "Hi, Tanya."

"Hi. I'm sure you know why I'm calling."

"Probably. Are you recording this?"

"No. You know I wouldn't do that without asking first. Can you comment?"

"About what?"

She sighed. "Rachel, let's not play games. You know what. The shooting at Daniels Industries. We have three eyewitnesses who say you were involved. Two call you a hero."

"That's a gross exaggeration."

"Possibly, but that's their words, not mine. Can you say what happened?"

"What do the police say?"

"Very little. They haven't released names or any information as to what happened or why. Was one of the men your client?"

"I can't say."

"Can't or won't?"

"Can't. You know I'd tell you if I could. All I can say is, I was there."

"You can't say why?"

"'Fraid not."

"Look, we air in five minutes and this is our lead story. Give me something. Will you confirm Warren Daniels shot Steven Raines, his chief financial officer?"

"Sorry, Tanya. If the police aren't giving out names, I can't either. Do you know if the victim is alive or not?"

"Out of surgery but critical is all the hospital will say and they're not saying who he is either. However, our witnesses named both him and the shooter. Was it personal or business related? We've heard hints of an affair with Mrs. Daniels."

"I really can't say. Wish I could help but can't."

"All right. Thanks anyway."

"Hold on a sec. I'd recheck your so-called eyewitnesses, if I were you. Strictly off the record, the door was closed. There are no eyewitnesses other than the three people in the room and we're not talking."

"Got it. Have ta run. Bye."

I put the phone down and picked up the TV remote on the coffee table. "Grab a seat ladies, I think I'm going to be on TV."

Eight

Terry and Paula met for dinner at Belle's Diner. As usual, Terry spent most of his day across the street at the JoAnne Frances Hanson Memorial Library surfing the net and her-his friends' accounts looking for new information on his-her family's murders. Terry was slowly getting used to his-her gender identity.

They were settled in a booth enjoying burgers with fries and chocolate shakes when the Channel 3 Six O'Clock Report started on the television on the wall behind the counter. The sound was off and closed captioning scrolled across the bottom of the screen.

The lead story involved a shooting at a local manufacturing plant. The shooter and victim weren't named, but local private investigator Rachel Cord was mentioned twice along with her picture. No information was given as a reason for the shooting. That story was followed by a five-car pile-up on the interstate involving a tractor-trailer that tied up traffic for several hours. No deaths were reported but eight people, including two children, were transported to local hospitals. Other stories dealt with the mayor, local events and the president's latest rants and tweets against the Democrats and the media.

Paula glanced over at the changing pictures now and then but paid little attention to the closed captioning. Just before the first break pictures of Tessa Ryker, the Ryker farmhouse, and the Ryker family came up behind the female news anchor.

"Tess. Look." Paula said.

"I'm Terry, remember?" he whispered back.

"Sorry. I forgot. But look." Paula pointed.

Terry turned. The television was muted but he caught the last bit of the closed captioning scroll.

" . . . *Blank County, Nebraska, Sheriff Baxter Donahue earlier today right after these messages.*"

Terry turned back. "I need to hear this."

"Isn't he — ?"

"Yes."

"Susie?" Paula called out. "Can you turn the sound up on the TV? We'd like to hear the news."

"Sure thing."

The waitress wearing the *Susie Q* nametag picked up a remote and the television's sound came on. Paula kept eating through the commercials, but Terry's eyes were glued to the screen.

When the Channel 3 logo appeared indicating the end of the break, Terry moved to a counter stool, his supper forgotten. The lead camera focused on news anchor Tanya Waverly.

"Welcome back. Just over two weeks ago, October eighth, at high noon at a quiet farmhouse outside of Hartfield, Nebraska, a family was torn apart by brutal and callous murder. The bodies of the father, Ronald Terrence Ryker; the mother, Caroline Alice Ryker; and eight-year-old Katrina April Ryker were discovered by police the following day. Missing was fourteen-year-old Tessa Anne Ryker."

A picture of the Ryker family and one of Tessa were inset on the screen behind Waverly. The family photograph was the same three-year-old one that sat on a table between Tessa's parents' chairs in their living room. Tessa's photo was from last year's school yearbook. Tessa's face was fuller then than now. She'd lost the last of her baby fat since then. There was little resemblance between the picture and Terry's current leaner and short hair look.

Tears filled Tessa's eyes as she remembered finding her dead family and listened to Waverly.

"What exactly happened at the home and the whereabouts of Tessa Ryker are still mysteries. I spoke with Blank County Sheriff Baxter Donahue today in our studios on the current situation. Here is my exclusive Channel 3 interview."

"She's such a pretty girl, isn't she?" Susie had moved over to watch the TV report also. "They're saying she killed her family. Do you think she did it?"

Tessa blinked back tears. Remembered she was now Terry.

"No, ma'am," Terry choked out. "Don't believe it."

On screen, Waverly and Sheriff Donahue sat on comfortable side chairs half facing each other. A table with glasses of water was between them. Waverly wore the same blue jacket and dark blouse and slacks she wore as news anchor. Donahue was dressed comfortably in a tweed sports coat, blue broadcloth shirt, dark red tie, pressed jeans and boots. His tan, rugged looks and military short hair going gray at the temples gave him the look of quiet authority.

Terry's eyes burned with hatred.

"Sheriff Donahue, it's more than two weeks since the Ryker family murder and Tessa Ryker's disappearance. Do you know what happened that day?"

"We have lots of evidence but interpreting it correctly is an ongoing responsibility."

"Doesn't some of the evidence suggest Terry Ryker shot his family then killed himself?"

"Suggestion isn't established fact. The murder weapon is missing. It's well known the Rykers didn't keep guns. There are a lot of questions still to be answered."

"I thought all farms kept guns."

Donahue smiled. "Most but not all."

"Mr. Ryker served in Afghanistan and was wounded there. Didn't he suffer from PTSD? Could that explain why he might have killed them?"

"I can't say. His medical records are privileged information. I knew Terry and his family well. Our families have visited each other many times. Terry and I were in high school together. We served in the same Guard unit. We were together in Afghanistan until he was wounded and sent home. It's true he's had continual medical care, but the Terry Ryker I knew was stable and dependable. I'm not inclined to believe he'd do something like that."

"Is it possible the daughter, Tessa, was involved in her family's deaths?"

"We're exploring that possibility among others, but we can't know until we find and speak with her."

"Your county attorney has announced Tessa Ryker as a suspect. Why is that?"

"Wade Vanderhorn sometimes speaks before thinking. Tessa Ryker is a person of interest. Meaning we need to speak with her."

"It was first reported she might have been kidnapped. Is that still a working theory?"

"If she was, she managed to get away from her kidnapper. So far we've found no evidence to corroborate that one way or another. She skipped school that day, and from her phone's GPS history, we know she was in the area at the time of the murders. What we don't know is if she was involved or not or may possibly be a witness only."

"Our police say she was seen alone at the Greyhound station here late on the night of the murders."

"We only discovered that a few days ago, unfortunately."

"I understand that, but could she have gotten here that quickly after the killings?"

"Yes. Hartfield is about a seven-hour drive from here. No problem."

"She's only fourteen. Does she know how to drive?"

"She drives tractors and farm vehicles regularly. A Ford one-fifty would be no problem."

"She hasn't contacted any authorities, has she?"

"No, she has not."

"Doesn't that suggest she may have been involved?"

"Not necessarily. I believe she's scared and doesn't know what to do."

"Do you think she may still be here?"

"This is a large city. I understand it attracts a lot of runaway teens. She may have met and be with some of them staying below the radar. So, yes, I think it's possible."

"There's a large reward for her return, isn't there?"

"Yes. The Nebraska Farmers Association and others have put together $40,000 for her safe return. As a result of that, we've had hundreds of tips and reported sightings as far afield as California, Key West and New York City. The sighting at the bus station is the first solid lead we or the FBI have had since she disappeared."

"How has this tragedy affected your community?"

"I'm not sure *grief-stricken* is a strong enough term." Donahue paused. "It's devastated everyone, including my department. Murder is uncommon in our area. A triple killing unheard of. The Rykers were well known and well liked. Rykers have farmed that land for more than a hundred years. They're an integral part of the community. They're family. Their loss is . . . unfathomable."

"Have funerals been planned?"

"Yes. A joint funeral and memorial service for Terry, Caroline and Katrina will be held Monday the twenty-eighth in Hartfield."

"Will you be going back to Blank County now?"

"Not right away. My team there is capable of handling the investigation and other duties. I'll be working with local authorities here the next few days in hopes of finding Tessa. I plan to be back in time for the funerals though."

"If Tessa is watching, what would you say to her?"

Donahue looked at the camera. Phone numbers appeared at the bottom of the screen.

"Tessa. Talk to us. Call the police here, call the FBI or call my department. We can help you. We want to help you. We need you to help us. Your family needs you to help us."

"Sheriff Donahue, thank you for speaking with us."

"Thank you for having me here."

The screen shifted back to Waverly at her anchor desk.

"It's been two weeks since this horrific tragedy occurred. Someone has seen or knows where Tessa Ryker is. If you have any information as to her whereabouts call any of the numbers displayed below or this station. Stay tuned for Sports with Bob Dale's prediction for tonight's second World Series game between the Astros and Nationals right after these messages."

"I sure hope she's okay," Susie said and looked around. "Not sure what I'd do if she came in here."

Terry looked at her. "Make her something to eat then call the police, I expect."

"I guess. Definitely feed her. Bet she's hungry and scared, poor thing. Hope she's somewhere safe and dry. Y'all need anything else."

"No, ma'am. We're good. Just the check, please."

"Comin' right up."

Terry went back and sat with Paula. His food was cold but he wasn't hungry any longer. Paula leaned forward.

"Are you okay?"

Terry brushed a tear from his cheek. "They're burying my family Monday."

"You can't be there, you know. You wouldn't be safe."

"No one will recognize me. Did you see that old picture they're using?"

"Maybe not here or most anywhere else. But in Hartfield? Where you grew up and lived until two weeks ago? A small town where everyone knows everyone? They all know you and they'll be looking closely at every stranger at the funeral."

"That's my family. I *have* to be there."

"I'm sorry. You can't. And that report's going to have people looking hard for you here. We need to get you to Colorado."

"Not yet. The sheriff is here. I need to get him to confess somehow."

"Are you really sure he did it? He didn't seem such a bad person on TV. Seemed like he really cared to hear what you have to say."

"He's a charmer, all right. But he's lying. I *saw* him. Saw him come out of our house. He killed my family. He'll kill me as soon as he gets the chance. I know it. And no one is going to believe me unless I get the proof he did it."

"How are you going to do that? You're fourteen."

Terry turned to the window and mumbled, "Don't know yet. I'll figure a way." He moved across the booth seat. "Let's get out of here. I'm not hungry."

Nine

"*Forty* **thousand dollars.** Are they kidding? I don't recall the sheriff mentioning *that* when he hired us." Barb's voice was full of sarcasm.

"You're right. He didn't. But that's not the point."

"The point?"

"Finding Tessa Ryker if she's still in the city."

Barb nodded but wasn't ready to give up. "Think we're eligible for the reward if we find her?"

"Reasonable question. Usually law enforcement isn't eligible for rewards. We're working for Sheriff Donahue, but he's paying us with personal funds not out of his county budget. We're not law enforcement. And he's not providing the reward, the farmers association is. If we find her—and that's an awfully big if right now—I suppose we could put in a claim. But let's not put the cart before the horse. We have to find her first."

The office phone rang and I answered it.

"Confidential Investigations. Rachel Cord speaking. How may I help you?"

"Hi, Rachel. It's Ariana Feldman. Bad news, I'm afraid. My people have checked all the homeless camps we work with. No one's seen the girl you're looking for."

"Thanks, Ariana."

"Of course we'll keep looking and asking."

"Thanks again. Have a good evening." I replaced the phone. "That was Ariana. No sightings. Jen? When can we start looking at the stuff you're gathering?"

"Now. The programs are still running and collecting anything new, but I can look through what's already filtered out."

"Will it be faster if we all go through it?"

"Not really."

"Rachel?" I turned to Barbara. "Jen's a whiz. She'll get it done quicker alone. You have to still be bothered by the Daniels shooting, anyway. Why don't you go home? I'll stay and work on the background checks and answer the phones if any of our contacts call about Tessa."

"Hey, who's the boss here?" They just smiled at me. "All right. Call if you need me."

Jennifer and Barbara worked quietly through the evening. Barbara finished four of the backlog of background checks while answering the phone numerous times. None of the callers reported seeing Tessa Ryker. Most asked about the reward. Barbara became so exasperated she switched the phones over to their night answering service and went back to working on another background check.

"I think I have something," Jennifer called out a little later.

"What?"

Barbara walked around the cubical panels and stared at Jennifer's five flat-screen computer monitors. Jennifer pointed to the middle monitor.

"On the sixteenth, *HildySpeaksTrue* tweeted '*Unbelievable! Say it's not true, Tess. Tommy's dad says, "Evidence proves Tessa Ryker killed her family."*'"

"Who's *HildySpeaksTrue* and who's Tommy?"

"Hildred Speaks is one of Tessa's friends and classmates. I think Tommy is Thomas Wagner a friend of Tessa's boyfriend

Brian Miller. He's one of the people who's friended me on Facebook."

"Wagner? Isn't that the name of Donahue's chief deputy?"

"Yes it is. Harold Wagner. He's one of the contacts the sheriff gave us. Tommy's his son."

"Why would Wagner release that? It's not what Donahue's saying."

"Maybe he didn't. Maybe it was just a comment he made at the dinner table and Tommy repeated it. Maybe even exaggerated it some. Or maybe the sheriff's not being straight with us. Anyway, that's not the important thing."

"No?"

"No. On the seventeenth, Hildy got this reply from CountryMom at BattleCreek-six-six-seventy-nine. *'It's a lie. Didn't do it.'*"

"Who's that?"

"Would you believe Tessa's mother?"

"What?"

"True. I went to CountryMom's Twitter site and from all the past tweets it's obvious it's Caroline Ryker's account. Also her birthdate is June six nineteen-seventy-nine."

"But she's dead. She was murdered on the eighth."

"I know. This is the only tweet since her death from her account. I think this is Tessa. I think she used her mom's account to reply. She's been real careful staying away from her own accounts and not posting to her friends, but when she saw Hildy's tweet, she just *had* to reply. She must know her mom's login and used that."

"You really think she sent this?"

"Definitely."

"We need to let the sheriff and Detectives Anderson and Kern know so they can trace where it came from."

"Maybe we shouldn't."

"What do you mean?"

"I've been thinking about this all evening while looking at this stuff. I'm sure it's her saying she didn't do it. Her friends all think she's innocent. Where did the gun come from if the Rykers didn't own any? And the sheriff—"

"What about him?"

"I don't know. Something Rachel said earlier."

"What?"

"That the sheriff is paying us out of his own pocket. Why would he do that? Why would he hire private investigators to begin with? He's got his own people, police in several states and the FBI looking. Why hire us? It doesn't make sense to me."

"He told us he's thinking outside the box. Thinks maybe we have contacts the police don't. He was a family friend. He personally cares about the girl. You could see it in his interview tonight."

"Maybe, but—"

"Besides, the sheriff's office can get the warrants to trace where she was when she sent that tweet. We can't. It's the only lead we have right now."

"Actually, we can trace it."

"How?

"Remember that beta program I mentioned to Rachel?"

"Jen! That's illegal and you know it. Rachel would skin us alive."

"Not if we don't tell her right away. And she'd forgive us if we find Tessa."

"Jen—"

"No, listen, Barb. That tweet was a week ago. It could have been sent from anywhere. Tessa may not even be here anymore. The program will tell us that. If it came from Denver or Nashville say, or who knows where, we could forget it and pass the tweet on to the sheriff's detectives. Let them handle it. Pretend we didn't trace it. Maybe they've caught it already and checked it out. You thought of that? No harm. No foul. But—"

"Jen, we can't—"

"*But,* if it *was* sent from here, we'd know she was still in the city a week ago. Could still be here. It'll give us direction and stop spinning our wheels."

"We can't do it. It's illegal."

Jennifer looked shamefaced and pointed to the end monitor. "I'm already running it."

"You didn't."

"I did. Look. It's found her." Jennifer checked the results. "She's here. Or to be specific, she was here on the seventeenth."

"Where?"

"The tweet was sent from the Hanson branch library."

"Where's that?"

Jennifer switched to another monitor, opened Firefox and called up Google Maps.

"Twenty-ninety-five Radford Avenue. Corner of Radford and Twenty-First Street. It's closed now but opens tomorrow at nine. We could check it out first thing in the morning."

"We? Thought you didn't want to be a field agent. And don't you need to be at work tomorrow?"

"I'll take the day off."

"You're not licensed."

"But you are. I'll be your assistant."

"Rachel's going to kill us when she finds out you used that program."

Jennifer switched back to the end monitor. Rapidly worked the keyboard. The program disappeared and the screen blinked several times then went dark. Jennifer turned back to Barbara.

"What program? I deleted it from the system, cleared history and any other trace of it. Who's driving tomorrow? You or me?"

Barb was right that the Daniels shooting weighed heavily on me. It bothered me most of the evening. Thoughts of finding Tessa Ryker were put aside. I felt confident that Barb and Jen would let me know if anything significant came up.

Wendy had watched the six o'clock news. She carefully listened as I spilled my guilt about letting Daniels shoot Raines. She kept reiterating it wasn't my fault. Reminded me not to take blame for things I can't control. She was right, but it's a habit I've never shaken.

I picked at my supper, hardly eating, even though Wendy had ordered my favorite Thai dish, Drunken Noodles. I changed to shorts and a tee, went to our home gym, opened the sliding glass doors to remove reflections and stared at the river as I mounted the treadmill and walked.

I like walking. It gives me time to think, clear my head. I've been a walker most of my life. Walk everywhere. For years I'd walk the 12 blocks to my office often stopping at Ladies Only, my go-to massage and fitness center, where I could relax under the skillful hands of Gretchen Neuhaus. Or walk to Phil's or Charlie's to eat or be with friends. I'd often walk up River Drive as far as the end of Riverside Park and back considering it just a good stretch of the legs and mind.

As I've gotten older, I spend more time on this treadmill than I do walking the streets. It's still time spent trying to work a problem, but more often—it seems—it's time spent trying to forget mistakes and staring at the broad river that rolls along with no concern for what lurks in the muck and mire of its depths.

"Rachel? It's nearly ten, do you want to watch the late news?"

"Already? Thanks. Be right there."

The best part of the news was that Steven Raines' condition had been upgraded to stable. His and Warren Daniels' names had been released. Daniels was being charged with attempted murder and held for arraignment. I was mentioned again, this time with details of my tackling Daniels and taking the gun from him and my attempts to keep Raines alive until the EMTs arrived.

I had no idea where that information came from. I doubted Daniels or Raines talked to the media, and I sure didn't. The only other source was my statement to the police. Have to check that out with Denise. I'm sure she wouldn't appreciate a leak in her department. If I had to pick who it was, I'd choose Det. Cassidy, but that could just be me being petty. It could be anyone who had access to my statement.

Tanya's interview with Sheriff Donahue was repeated with the addition that the station had already received more than 30 calls claiming to know where Tessa Ryker was. Those leads had been passed on to the police.

Wendy shut off the television. "Think any of those claims are real?"

"Anything's possible. I'm glad it's the police who have to verify them, not us. None of our contacts have confirmed a sighting yet, and I've had no calls tonight. Have to see if Barb and Jen made any progress in the morning. I told Sheriff Donahue I'd have something for him even if it isn't good."

"You feeling any better about Daniels and Raines?"

"Not better but I'm getting over the guilt complex."

"How 'bout a hot bubble bath? Would that help?"

"Together?"

"Of course together, Silly."

The surge of the Jacuzzi jets and the lavender-scented froth was totally relaxing. My back was to Wendy as I sat between her legs, my arms resting on her knees. Her hands kneaded my neck and shoulders. Then her thumbs ran along my spine as her hands worked down to the small of my back. She used her fists and fingers to knead and poke away my tightness.

"Mmmm. That feels great."

Wendy worked her way back up to my neck. "Better than Gretchen?"

"Different. Her touch is professional. Yours is . . ." I ran my nails along the outside of her legs up to her hips, "sexier."

"Ooh. Someone's getting frisky."

Wendy's hands slid around to caress my breasts. I leaned back against her as she kissed the nape of my neck.

Ten

Paula tried all evening to convince Terry it was time to head for Colorado and take up his new life.

"It's too dangerous to stay here any longer. That reward announcement will have everyone out looking for you."

"They'll be looking for Tessa Ryker not Terry Romer. I appreciate your concern. Really I do, but the sheriff's here. Now. I need time to think what to do. Please."

Paula shook her head. "Don't take too long thinking and don't do anything foolish. I need to get ready for work."

As Paula took her shower, Terry felt totally lost. Paula was right. *I'm 14, not the 19 on my driver's license. What can I possibly do to prove the sheriff guilty? Who would believe me if I said he did it?*

In frustration he turned on the television to catch Channel 3's *Late Night Report*. The Sheriff Donahue interview was repeated. Terry learned nothing new from that but a story on a shooting caught his interest. Private detective. He looked toward the closet where his bag of money lay. *Could I hire one? Would that one on TV —*

Paula came out of the bedroom. "Anything interesting?"

"Not really. Mostly repeats from earlier." Terry turned off the television. "Maybe I'll put on a movie later. Watch *The Grinch* again or something."

"Look. I don't want to argue. I'm only thinking of your best interest."

"I know and I appreciate it. I know you're right. Part of me's scared of going off alone even though you and your group have set things up for me. I've liked being here with you. It makes me feel safe. But I don't want the sheriff to get away with murder. He killed my parents—my sister. It's not right he get away with it."

"No, it's not right. But you're the only witness. The only one who knows he did it. Until you find a way for someone in authority to believe you, to look for other evidence, you need to hide; and right now, I believe Colorado as Terry Romer is the safest and best place for you."

"I'm sure you're right."

"You going to be okay tonight."

"Yes. Don't worry. I'll be fine. See you in the morning."

"Okay. G'night."

Terry made a snack and turned the television back on. He flipped channels spending only minutes checking different movies and programs not finding anything of interest. His mind elsewhere.

He glanced at the clock: 11:22. Paula should be safely at work. He turned off the television and took his duffel from the closet. He choked back his anger as he picked up the towel-wrapped gun—the gun that had killed his family. The image of his father on the floor dead, the gun in his left hand, overwhelmed Terry, and with tears flowing, he became Tessa again for a moment. Wiping the tears away he set the gun aside. He looked at the bundles of money in the bottom of the bag.

Is this what it's all about? Why? What good is it? He felt the urge again to get rid of it. Burn it. Bury it. Throw it in a dumpster or the river.

He calmed down. No, use it to catch the sheriff. What's a detective cost? Thousands probably.

Terry took out $5,000 and put it in his backpack. He replaced the gun and stashed his sports duffel back in the closet. He opened his laptop and logged onto Paula's Wi-Fi connection. He'd promised Paula he wouldn't log into any of Tessa's accounts or any of her friends' accounts. What he was looking for wouldn't violate that promise. He googled *private detective* then clicked on *The BEST 10 Private Investigators Near You.*

The search took him to *Yelp* where only a couple of the listings had reviews. Those reviews ran the gamut of 5-star raves to completely unsatisfied 1-stars for the same agency. So how do you choose? He clicked on two websites, but the investigators were former police detectives. No way. They'd turn me in right away. I don't see that woman from the news.

Remembering her name, he opened a new tab and typed in *Rachel Cord*. There were millions of results including Facebook and LinkedIn profiles. He added *Private Investigator* to narrow the search and saw a picture of the woman he'd seen and links to many news articles and even books about her as well as to her business *Confidential Investigations*. That looked familiar. Terry went back to the *Yelp* tab. There it was, number nine on the list but there were no reviews. He clicked on the company's website link which opened in a new tab.

Confidential Investigations LLC *is a full service private investigation agency. Our services are available to private individuals, the legal profession and commercial clients.*

Confidential Investigations *will handle your case efficiently and quickly and provides the highest level of confidentiality.*

"Our clients come first and foremost. We work for you."

Terry hesitated clicking on the *Contact* link. He spent the next three hours reading the news articles and random parts of one book he downloaded about Rachel Cord. He wasn't sure what to do. Would this woman help him? Could he trust her or would she turn him in for the reward?

He thought some of the book he downloaded read more like the kind of thriller his mom liked than the memoir it claimed to be. It had been co-authored by Cord and a reporter named Andy Walther who worked for the *Daily Record*, the local paper. Did these things really happen to her? It was hard to believe. Nothing like that ever happened to Mom's favorite detective, Kinsey Millhone.

One incident described Cord taking out a phony cop using only a rolled up magazine. Would that really work?

Terry picked up one of Paula's magazines, rolled it tightly and held it as described in the book. The ends protruded from both sides of his fist. He hit the palm of his other hand hard. Ouch! That hurt. He smiled as he thought of jamming it into Sheriff Donahue's gut.

He went back to the *Confidential Investigations* link and clicked the *Contact* button. The contact page listed three choices: telephone #(24-hour service), email, and address (Mann Avenue Plaza, 1205 Mann Ave, Room 222 West). Terry chewed his lower lip debating, hesitating. He yawned then glanced at the time in the corner of the screen: 2:45 a.m. Way too tired. Can't decide now. Think about it in the morning. He quit Firefox, shutdown and put the laptop back in his backpack. As an afterthought, he put the rolled-up magazine in the backpack too.

Eleven

Barbara parked her red Miata convertible at the JoAnne Frances Hanson Memorial Library shortly after 8:00 a.m.

"Why are we here so early," Jennifer asked. "The library doesn't open till nine."

"Like you, I went to Google Maps then checked out the area. There's a convenience store and a diner right across the street. If it was Tessa who sent that Twitter reply from here, there's a good chance she's been in the store, the diner or both. Let's go have breakfast and see if anyone remembers her."

Belle's Diner was busy with the breakfast rush that kept three waitresses hopping. The place was like a '50s diner: booths with red Naugahyde upholstery along the front windows; long counter with stools; circular pie display by the cash register; chrome-plated mini song selectors along the counter; a Wurlitzer jukebox at the far end by the bathrooms playing, *Tell Laura I Love Her*.

Barbara and Jennifer looked at a menu while they waited for a booth to be cleared. When they were seated Barbara ordered the Veggie Omelet with tomato, onion, green pepper, mushroom and spinach with whole-wheat toast and a cup of fresh fruit as her side.

"Do you have tomato juice?"

"We're out," said the waitress whose nametag was *Susie Q*. "We have V8 and Tasty Tom."

"I'll have the V8 and coffee, thank you."

Jennifer was tempted by the all-you-can-eat hotcake special but finally decided on the Belgian Waffle with strawberry topping and whipped cream as well as two eggs over easy and a double order of crisp bacon. She ordered coffee with cream and a glass of water.

The waitress noticed Jennifer's sweatshirt. "My daughter goes to Cramer. Wonder if you know her?"

"Probably not. I graduated five years ago."

"Really? You can't be more than twenty."

"Thanks. I turned twenty-seven last month. What's your daughter studying?"

"This time? Journalism with a minor in lazy." They all laughed.

As the waitress walked away to fill their order, Barbara shook her head.

"I'll never understand how you stay so slim with what you eat."

"Clean living." Jennifer smirked. "Also I fast on Sundays."

Barbara rolled her eyes. "You've never fasted a day in your life. As for clean living . . ." Barbara waggled one hand back and forth.

Jennifer laughed. "True. I don't know. Great metabolism, I guess. Food's never been a problem."

By the time they finished eating the rush was over. All that were left was a couple in the corner booth, three businessmen who just arrived in another booth, and an elderly man still sitting at the counter. Jennifer glanced out the window and saw more cars in the library parking lot and a group of people gathered near the doors.

Their waitress came over with a coffeepot. "Would you ladies like a refill?"

Barbara pushed her cup over. "Yes, thank you."

"Me too, please, and I'll need more cream. I could also go for another waffle." Jennifer saw Barbara's look. "On second thought, I better not. Just the coffee, thanks."

The waitress refilled their cups and laid three creamers on the table.

Jennifer pointed to her nametag. "Is your name really Susie Q?"

"Not really. It's Beverly. The owner thought it would be cute if our nametags were the same as women in fifties' song titles. It fits the diner theme, and all of those songs are on the jukebox, but it can get confusing at times."

"I'm Jennifer, and this is my colleague, Barbara. We're hoping you and the other waitresses can help us."

"How's that?"

Barbara took out a picture of Tessa Ryker. It was the same photograph that appeared on Channel 3.

"We're private investigators hired to try to locate this girl." Barbara handed her a business card along with the photo. "Has she been in here at any time in the past two weeks?"

"That's the girl I saw on the news last night. Teresa something."

"Tessa Ryker."

"That's right. She looks familiar but that's probably because I've seen her picture on TV so much. I haven't seen her in here. I mostly work the evening shift. I'm only helping out this morning because Rhonda called in sick. No, sorry, I'm sure this girl hasn't been in when I've been on. You think she's around here somewhere?"

"It's possible and this is a popular eatery."

"That's true. We do stay busy." Beverly called over her shoulder. "Donna? Have you seen this girl? Donna's one of the few of us whose real name matches her nametag."

Donna came over and looked at the picture. Shook her head. "Pretty girl. Terrible thing what happened to her family, isn't it? No, don't think I've seen her. Let me ask Inez."

She took the photograph to the counter. The waitress there whose nametag was *Lola* looked at it and also shook her head.

"Never seen her. Sorry."

The elderly man looked at the photo too. "Sure. She was here. Two weeks ago."

Barbara quickly moved to the counter. "Are you sure about that, sir?"

"Darn tootin'. No doubt about it."

"Jerry," Donna warned. "Don't go makin' up stories just to flatter these young ladies."

"Humph! Would I do that?"

"Is the Pope Catholic?"

"Jerry's pushing eighty," Beverly said quietly to Jennifer. "He's here most days but tends to play loose with the truth."

"Can you recall when you saw her, sir?" Barbara pointed to the photograph.

"Course I can. I'm old, not senile. Though she didn't look like she does in this picture."

"She didn't?"

"Nah. She had on a baseball cap covering her hair and was wearin' one of those puffy parkas and black-framed readers. I got a pair just like 'em."

The mention of the parka and glasses got Barbara excited. That's what Tessa had been wearing at the bus station.

"When was she here?"

"Let's see. It was real early. Shortly after Rhonda opened up. I had my coffee and was waitin' for my biscuit. I like 'em hot just outta the oven with lots of butter. It was Monday, two weeks ago."

Barbara's excitement waned. Monday two weeks ago was Oct. 7th, before the murders.

"Jerry, you're wrong." Lola said. "I open Mondays and you weren't here."

"You sure you're not stretchin' it, Jerry?" Donna asked.

Jerry's face colored. "I know what I saw. Rhonda opened. Juanita was in the back makin' a fresh rack of biscuits. Mickey and Hank was here too."

"Rhonda opens Wednesdays and Thursdays," Beverly said. "That's why I'm here this morning."

"Miss?"

Beverly turned to the couple in the corner.

"May we have our check?"

"Excuse me, gotta take care of this."

"Could it have been Wednesday morning, sir? The ninth?" Barbara asked.

"Coulda been, I guess. Woulda sworn it was Monday though. She sat alone back there in the corner facing the window."

"How can you be sure it was this girl the way she was dressed?"

Jerry's eyes narrowed. "Don't believe me, do ya?"

"I'm not saying that, sir. I'm hoping you're right. I'm sure you are. I just want to verify how you recognized her."

"From the news. I watch all the news channels and the local broadcasts and read the papers. Been following this story closely. Think something's fishy there. Anyway, they showed pictures of her at the bus station the other night. That's how she was dressed except for the Cardinals cap. The red one. Didn't have that in those pictures. Just didn't make the connection until you asked just now."

A bell dinged at the kitchen window. "Order up." Lola picked up two plates and handed them to Donna who took them to the businessmen's booth. Donna returned and got the third plate Lola passed her.

Barbara's tension eased. "Did you see her leave?"

"Nah. I left 'fore she did. She ordered a big breakfast just like your friend there."

"Excuse us, please." The couple from the corner edged their way past and left.

"Thanks for stoppin' in. Have a good day," Donna said as she rejoined the discussion. "You know, I think I remember who Jerry means, but I don't think she looked anything like this picture. I don't think it was her."

"Humph! You wouldn't recognize—"

"Watch your tongue, Jerry," Lola warned, "or we'll ban you for a month."

"Humph!"

"I mean it, Jerry."

"Yeah. Yeah. I hear ya. How 'bout some more coffee?"

"Comin' right up."

"What did the girl look like?" Barbara asked Donna.

"Pretty much as Jerry said. Baseball cap, parka and black-rimmed glasses. You see I was late that morning. I usually start at six and was running behind. The girl had finished eating by the time I'd started, but she wasn't ready to leave. Seemed to me she was waiting for someone. I refilled her coffee cup a couple of times. She was real polite but quiet. When the other girl joined her, she ordered another strawberry waffle."

"Who joined her?"

"I don't know her name. She's comes in fairly often just after seven. She's been in a couple times since then. Alone though. Not with that other girl. I think she works late nights nearby. Always orders the same thing, coffee, juice and a toasted bagel with cream cheese. She paid for both of them."

"Cash or credit card?"

"Cash. Left a nice tip now that I remember."

"What did she look like?"

"Early to mid twenties. Pretty ordinary, really, except for some piercings and her hair's a sort of purply red and cut like that Three Stooges guy."

"I know her," Beverly said. "That's Paula. She works the midnight shift at that twenty-four hour Walgreens up the street. Stops by for dinner once or twice a week. She was in last night with her cousin."

"What cousin?"

"Nice looking guy if you like the lean and hungry type. Name's Terry. Paula said he was visiting from somewhere in Colorado. Golden or Boulder, maybe. Somewhere near Denver, anyway."

"Do you know Paula's full name, where she lives?"

"No, sorry."

"That's okay. We can check at Walgreens. Thank you ladies, you've been a big help."

"What about me? I'm the one said she was in here in the first place."

"You're right, sir, you did. Thank you. You were a great help."

"Darn tootin'. Will I get some of that reward they're offerin' when you find her?"

"We're not connected with that, but if you'll give me your full name and address, I'll be happy to pass it along with the information you've given to the proper authorities."

"Can't I stay anonymous?"

"You can, but how will anyone contact you about the reward?"

Jerry seemed to give that a lot of thought. Beverly said quietly to Jennifer, "Jerry doesn't trust *Big Brother* as he calls anything connected to the government."

"You got a card?" Barbara handed him one. "When they find the girl, I'll check back with you ta see if my info made it happen. I can claim some of that reward then, can't I?"

Barbara smiled. "You've got a deal, sir. We'll keep your name secret till then. Thanks for your help. Beverly, guess we should pay our bill and get going."

"You know what bothers me?" Donna asked the room. "I can't believe that sweet girl killed her family, so why hasn't she gone to the police?"

"Simple. They're the ones that killed 'em."

Everyone turned to Jerry.

"Stands to reason, if you ask me," he continued. "The father served in Afghanistan, didn't he? He must've found out something that'd put the kibosh on us being over there, and the CIA or Black Ops—some part of the secret government cabal, anyway—tried to kill him then. But he was only wounded and sent home pretty messed in the head. He prob'ly recently remembered, and they had to kill him and his family to keep him from revealing what it was. It's all because of special interests and the military-industrial complex. War is profitable. Peace ain't. That's why they killed the Kennedys too, you know back then. It weren't Oswald or that Sirhan fella they pinned it on."

All three waitresses began arguing with Jerry about his conspiracies. Barbara and Jennifer rolled their eyes as they headed for the door. Outside, Jennifer turned to Barbara.

"You think Jerry's on to something?"

"Maybe *on* something," Barbara laughed. "He's definitely anti-government and probably filled with every ridiculous and implausible theory out there."

"But did he really see Tessa?"

"Yes, I think so. Donna's description matches his and it's how she appeared on the bus station video minus the baseball cap."

Jennifer looked toward the library. The crowd was gone and one person came out with an armload of books.

"So, which first? Library or Walgreens?"

"Convenience store first, then library then Walgreens."

Twelve

Mary Farr was at the reception desk at the top of the stairs when I arrived.

"Morning, Rachel. I saw the news about the shooting. Were you hurt?"

"Just my pride, Mary. Have you seen Barb this morning? All I get is her voicemail. It's not like her to leave her phone off."

"Haven't seen her. There were five reports on my desk to go out with the mail when I came in. She must have left them last night. Maybe she's taking comp time for working late."

"Maybe. Any calls?"

"Not this morning. Your night service said they had three calls with negative reports on Tessa Ryker. Here's who called. Want the phones transferred back to your office?"

"Yes, please. I'll answer them. See you later."

How late had they worked last night? If she wanted to take time off, why hadn't Barb let me know? Strange. She knows we're under a tight deadline. She was there when I told Sheriff Donahue we'd have something for him today.

I entered my private office. On my desk was a note from Barb and copies of the five background checks she had completed last night. That put a big dent in our backlog. There was also a list of our contacts that called about Tessa Ryker.

None had seen the girl. I added the three names Mary gave me.

Barb's note said they quit at 11:00 and she'd started a draft report for Donahue. She left me the file link to access it. There wouldn't be much there. All the news was negative so far. I'd probably be telling the sheriff he was wasting his money. All together, we'd already clocked more hours than the retainer covered with little if not nothing to show for it.

The last sentence in Barb's note was puzzling. *I'll be late coming in, there's maybe a slight lead I want to check out.*

What's *maybe a slight lead*? How *slight* does a lead need to be to be a *maybe*? A lead's a lead whether it pans out or not. No maybes about it. And why didn't she say what it was and where she was going? She usually keeps me better informed — if for no other reason than so I can cover her butt.

Why is her phone off? I had a problem with that years ago. Always forgetting to turn mine on. Thought cellphones were more bother than what they were worth back then. But Barb grew up with the damn things. It's like her iPad is part of her. She's never without it and it's *never* off. So why doesn't she answer my voice messages and texts?

I went to the other half of the office. Jen's computers were quietly chugging along gathering and filtering new data on Tessa's friends most likely. Barb's desk was clear and the drawers locked. Wonder if she told Jen where she was going? The office phone rang.

"Confidential Investigations. Rachel Cord speaking. May I help you?"

"Is Barbara Lange in?"

"She's out on assignment. May I help?"

"I'm Teri Underwood from the Salvation Army Thrift Store on South Main."

"Yes?"

"Barbara and I are old friends. She called me yesterday about that missing girl, Tessa Ryker. She thought maybe the girl would try to get new clothes and dump her old stuff."

"And did you find something?"

"Yes. This morning. I was sorting stuff from one of our collection bins and came across a pink sports bag. Inside it was some clothes and a rolled up Army duffel bag. R. T. Ryker and a serial number were stenciled on it. Do you think it's connected with the girl?"

"Yes I do. Do you still have the stuff?"

"Yes. I put it all aside in the office in case Barbara thought it was important."

"It's very important, Ms. Underwood. Could I come get it?"

"Yes, certainly."

"Where are you exactly?"

"We're a block west of the Amtrak station in Old Town. You can't miss us."

"I know where that is. I can be there in half an hour. Would that be all right?"

"That's fine. If I'm not at the register just ask for me."

"Okay. See you soon. Thank you for calling us."

I should have called Sgt. Wainwright from Missing Persons and let him collect the bag. This was evidence. He had the forensic means to glean anything useful from the stuff Tessa dumped. But I didn't feel we'd really earned Donahue's fee yet, and this was the best lead we had.

I scribbled a note for Barb and left it on her desk. At least *I* keep my colleagues informed. I put a couple pair of vinyl gloves in my bag and locked up. Both Mary and Doris were at the reception station.

"I need to go out. Can you catch the phones?"

"No problem," Doris said.

I stopped at the head of the stairs and turned back.

"Do you have a large, clean trash bag I could have?"

"Sure." Doris said. "What size? The thirteen gallon or the thirty-three?"

"The thirty-three."

"I'll get one from the supply closet."

"If Barb comes in before I get back, tell her to turn her phone on and call me." Mary gave me a cheesy grin. "What?"

"Just remembering how often we had to remind you years ago."

"That was then and this is now. I'm supposed to be the boss and know what's happening."

"Of course you are."

"Sarcasm noted. Thanks, Doris, for the trash bag."

With bag and gloves to keep from contaminating possible evidence, I headed out. Old Town and the Amtrak station was a straight shot north on Central Boulevard from my office. My mouth watered as I passed Charlie's Chicago Hot Dog Stand at the corner of Central and Cutter Avenue. The thought of one of his chili and slaw dogs was enticing even though it was only 9:30 in the morning. Maybe I'd stop on the way back.

The city is mostly laid out in a grid with streets and boulevards going north-south and avenues going east-west. Most of the streets are numbered going higher west from the river, while most of the avenues are named. The biggest exceptions are North and South Main Streets that run east-west parallel to and on each side of the railroad tracks. They were both called Main Street before the current system went into effect and their north and south designations indicated their positions relative to the tracks. This is often confusing to newcomers and tourists.

There was little traffic, the lights were with me, and my BMW gave me no problems though I still missed my old Geo Prizm that I'd had forever. It was a better car for surveillance but was needing repairs too often and I got a good deal on the used Beamer.

I arrived sooner than I expected. Teri Underwood showed me the items she had put aside. I used the vinyl gloves to avoid contaminating potential evidence. There was the Army duffel with Ryker's name, Tessa's pink sports bag, her puffy parka, a few tops, a couple pair of jeans and a worn pair of cross trainers with pink edging and laces. There was nothing that immediately told me where Tessa was or what she was currently wearing.

"Everything was stuffed in this sports bag?"

Teri nodded. "Yes. I didn't make the connection until I saw Ryker's name on the duffel."

"And this was found in one of your collection boxes?"

"Yes. The one near the bus stops at Westbrook Mall."

"When was that box emptied?"

"That one's usually emptied every Monday morning. It gets a lot of donations. Especially on the weekends. When it's full people will just pile stuff next to it. When that happens we get called and have to make an extra pick-up. There are some bins we let go a couple weeks before emptying but not that one. We've had a lot of stuff come in this week, and I didn't get to sorting this lot until this morning."

"So this bag could have been dropped off any time between . . ." I thought for a moment, "between Monday the fourteenth and this past Monday."

"Actually Tuesday the fifteenth. We didn't pick up the fourteenth because of Columbus Day. And it would have had to be dropped off before nine a.m. this Monday. I checked our pick-up log and that's when we emptied that bin."

"If she dropped this stuff off way up there, I doubt she came in here before to buy other clothing."

"Doesn't seem likely, does it? Not much help then, I guess."

"I wouldn't say that. It's a lead we didn't have before. I'll give you a receipt for everything and make sure this gets to the proper authorities."

Westbrook Mall is located on North Ferry Avenue, a major east-west artery on the north side of the city. Several bus routes end there. The mall's heyday was at least ten years ago. It's one of those old-fashioned labyrinthine malls with limited access hopefully surrounded by a sea of cars. Two anchors and several other stores have closed without being replaced. The Cineplex-14, the food court and some specialty shops are mainly what keep it going. There's a lot of talk of either updating the mall or tearing it down and starting fresh but nothing definite has begun.

I was on good terms with mall security. Over the years their surveillance cameras have helped me locate many missing juveniles. I called ahead and Dennis Cobb, chief of mall security, said he'd have a fresh cup of coffee waiting for me.

Cobb is former police. He spent his entire 20-year career in uniform and on the streets. He took over as chief of security at Westbrook seven years ago. He reminds me a lot of my old friend and father figure, homicide detective Frank Taylor. Both are big black men with laid-back personalities and sarcastic senses of humor. Taylor retired in 2010, and he and his wife Lorraine went back to his hometown, Chicago. We still talk on the phone, exchange letters and cards, and Wendy and I have visited them twice. It's about time for another visit. Maybe they'd like to come down here this time. Have to call and ask. Since neither the Cubs nor the White Sox made it to the World Series this year, Frank won't be in a frazzle over who wins.

"Where's my hot dog?" a deep rich voice complained as I entered the mall security office.

I've often told Cobb he should be on the radio or TV with that voice. He said it wasn't his style, but I was always welcome to come hear him sing with the Tabernacle Baptist Church choir. I keep meaning to but haven't made it yet.

As for his hot dog, he has a penchant for Charlie's Chicago-style hot dogs that is only exceeded by Taylor's. Something else the two have in common. Frank Taylor would easily eat two at a time and twice a day if Lorraine didn't keep after him. There were numerous times we'd lunch at Charlie's luxuriating over a hot dog discussing cases, problems and life in general. I sorely miss those days.

I don't begrudge either their desire. Charlie's version of the definitive Chicago hot dog is a vision of heaven. A grilled oversized all-beef hot dog nestled in a toasted poppy-seed bun surrounded by neon green relish, diced onions, chopped cucumber, tomato wedges, mild Golden Greek peppers, and yellow mustard with a dash of celery salt. When I know I'm coming to the mall, I always bring a half dozen for Cobb and any of his crew that are there.

"Sorry. I was at the Salvation Army store on South Main before I knew I had to come here. It was too late to go all the way back to Charlie's."

"If you were a block from here, it wouldn't have been to late to turn around and pick up a passel of dogs from Charlie's."

"Mea culpa. I promise, Denny, to remember next time."

"Yeah, right. Six months from now, most likely. But I bet you'll stop there later and have one yourself without a glimmer of regret or sympathy for us poor starving working stiffs."

I raised my hand in a Scout salute. "I swear I won't be stopping at Charlie's for one of his Chicago dogs."

"Uh-huh. Chili and slaw dog?" I blushed and he pointed. "Gotcha! Coffee's fresh. Grab a cup and take a load off."

I got the coffee and sat in the armchair next to his desk.

"Who you looking for this time, Rachel?"

"Tessa Ryker."

"You and everyone else. The cops have been here three times scouring our videos with nary a glimpse of her. They must think we're not eyeballing every teen girl that comes in trying to ID her. What makes you think you'll have better luck?"

"I may know something the cops don't yet. Tessa, or someone, dropped off all her stuff from Nebraska in the Salvation Army box out by the bus stops here."

"You thinking she looks different than her pictures or description?"

"Exactly. You still have cameras out by the bus stops?"

"We do, but we're having trouble with the whole system. It's been here longer than I have and needs updating. I've got maintenance constantly repairing cameras and lighting all over and there's no money in the budget to do it right."

"Things getting tight?"

"Tighter than a tick in a dog's ear. We got budget cuts up the yin-yang. Another four stores dropped their leases. We're under sixty percent occupancy. Management wants me to let two more people go."

"Ouch."

"Tell me about it. Management doesn't understand that just because stores are closing, we still need enough people to cover this whole complex. Especially on weekends. We're still crowded then. Luckily, I got three good people I'd hate to lose lined up to join the police department. If they make it into the academy, they'll make as much there as they do here and, once certified, they're looking at knocking down fifty K to start. It's better for them and, hopefully, I'll be looking to hire people instead of letting someone go. But that's not your problem. Come on. Let's see if we can find your girl."

Cobb led me into the monitor room. Thirty screens showing the mall and parking lots were being watched by two people. Each screen seemed to be handling four cameras as the view changed every few seconds. Several of the views were blank or filled with fuzz. One of the operators turned as we entered.

"Boss? We're still having problems with the cameras in the west lot and down by Dillard's."

"Maintenance says they're on it. Have we got eyes on the ground in those areas?"

"Yes, but it's leaving our rovers thin."

"Well, let's do what we can and hope nothing happens."

Cobb turned to four inactive monitors in the corner. He pressed return on a keyboard and the monitors lit up.

"You said the cameras out by the bus stops showing the Salvation Army box. What days we looking for?"

"October fifteenth starting around nine a.m. through this Monday morning at nine."

"Have a seat. This'll take a few minutes."

We spent an hour studying the archived video files. We saw the box emptied on the 15th but the best camera went dead shortly after and wasn't repaired until the next day. Another camera went out Saturday the 19th but wasn't repaired until after 10:00 a.m. on the 21st. Other cameras in the area weren't close enough to tell what was being dropped off, and we didn't see anyone dropping off a pink bag or that we thought could be Tessa Ryker.

"Looks like you wasted a trip, Rachel."

"As another security chief told me years ago, 'It is what it is.' Thanks, Denny, for trying. Next time I'll remember the hot dogs."

"Sure you will. At least feel a tinge of guilt while you enjoy that chili and slaw dog I *know* you're going to stop for."

I relished every single messy bite of Charlie's chili and slaw dog along with an order of fries without feeling a single modicum of guilt. That's because I had Charlie make up an order of a dozen of his Chicago dogs and two quarts of coleslaw then called We Deliver to take them to Denny and his crew. It pays to keep your contacts happy.

Thirteen

Terry sat on the low wall bordering the reading garden waiting for the library to open. Several others gathered near the door. Two vapers and a smoker conversed in smoke signals in a corner of the parking lot.

Terry stretched and yawned. He hadn't slept well. He tossed and turned most of the night plagued by the need to make a decision. He knew Paula was right. He was only fifteen. Okay, fourteen, but he'd be fifteen in December. The sensible thing to do was go to Colorado. Maybe even California or Hawaii. With the identity Anonymity provided and the cash hidden in Paula's closet he could go anywhere. Start a new life. But how could he with Sheriff Donahue out there getting away with murder?

The murder of *his* family. Tessa's family. The family being buried in four days and he couldn't be there for them. Terry pictured the sheriff at the gravesite looking sincere and caring, his arm around Aunt Beckie, comforting her.

No way in hell was *that* happening!

Terry looked up. Everyone was going in the library. He picked up his backpack and entered turning right as usual toward a sitting and reading area next to Café JoAnne, the concession and gift shop run by the Friends of the Library, and the large windows that overlooked the garden. Carrie and Christine, the two sisters that ran the cafe, reminded him of his mother and aunt. They were always friendly and recommending books to him.

"Have you read *Stranger in a Strange Land* by Robert Heinlein?" Carrie asked.

"No, I haven't. I'm still working my way through Harry Potter."

"It's a great book. Give it a try."

"I will. Thanks."

He bought a latte and a freshly baked chocolate chip cookie then sat in his regular spot, opened his laptop and connected to the library's free Wi-Fi.

In the interview the sheriff said he was staying in the area. But where? How do I find him? Does he have a planned agenda? Would the TV station or the police tell me? That Cord woman could probably find him. What then? Confront him with an empty gun? I don't dare use the bullets and clip I have. They're evidence. Can I buy others?

Munching on his cookie, Terry googled *"How old do you have to be to buy 9mm ammo?"* and was surprised to find a FOX News Investigates report on how easy is it for minors to buy gun ammunition that had 16-year-olds purchasing ammo without being asked for ID. Another link recommended telling the seller the ammo was for a rifle not for a handgun.

Were there 9mm rifles? He tried another search. Yes. Maybe getting ammo wouldn't be that hard. What about a replacement clip? He didn't find any definite restrictions.

He remembered a pawnshop across from the Walgreens where Paula worked advertised guns and supplies. Might as well give it a try. He packed his laptop and got up to leave.

"Leaving so soon?" Christine asked.

"Remembered an errand I need to do. I'll be back."

As Terry left, he held the door for two women entering. The one wearing a business suit and with her hair up was taller than him. The shorter one had her fair hair in a ponytail and was wearing a Cramer College sweatshirt and jeans.

"Thank you," the shorter one said.

"My pleasure, ma'am. Have a good day."

Terry stood nervously outside 21st Street Pawn & Loans. There were bars on the windows and door. He looked around but didn't see anyone watching him and there were no cars in the small lot. He decided he'd try buying the clip first then go somewhere else to buy the ammunition using the "it's for my rifle" ploy. He thought about what he was going to say, took a deep breath and entered the store.

A bell rang when he opened the door and a clerk came out from the back.

"Can I help you?"

"Yes. My dad's birthday is next week. He's a shooter. Goes to the range all the time. I was thinking of getting him an extra clip for his M9 Beretta. Do you have any?"

"That's the same as the 92FS, isn't it? Your dad in the military?"

"National Guard."

"Well thank him for his service for me. We got some over here. You want ten or fifteen round?"

"Which is better?"

"They're pretty much the same, but you don't have to reload as often with the fifteen."

"Ah, the fifteen then I guess."

"If your dad shoots a lot, two would be handier."

"How much are they?"

"The Beretta factory ones are $35 each, but the Mec-Gars are only $20. Some say they're better than the factory ones. I sell a lot of them."

"Okay. I'll take two of those."

"I'm sure your dad will appreciate it. What ammo does he use?"

"Ah?" Was this a trick question? "Nine millimeter?"

"I mean what brand? If it's his birthday, you might as well surprise him with some ammo too."

"I'm not sure. What do you recommend?"

"Well American Eagle and PMC are both popular for target shooting. They're inexpensive and both are 115 grain and full metal jackets. There's also Herter's which is a couple bucks cheaper a box. A lot of my customers are switching to that."

"I'll take a box of those."

"Cash or charge?"

"Cash."

A few minutes later, Terry stood outside the store still amazed he was able to buy everything he needed. He glanced around half expecting to get busted at any moment. Across the street at Walgreens, he saw the same two women that had been at the library get out of a red convertible with a black top. The shorter one saw him and waved. Terry sort of waved back and hurried south back toward the library.

He stopped at a bus stop a block later and sat on the bench. He opened the paper bag and looked at the two clips and the 50 round box of ammunition. Unbelievable. The guy didn't ask for ID and the bullets only cost ten bucks. Wow. Now all I need is to find you, sheriff. No way you're going to Trina's funeral. He put the bag in his backpack and took out the cell phone he'd bought and the phone numbers he'd written down.

He tried the television station first, but the person he spoke with couldn't tell him where Sheriff Donahue was and wanted him to leave his name and number if he had information on the missing Tessa Ryker. He hung up.

He started to call the police hotline number and stopped. Would the police get suspicious if I said I needed to talk only to the sheriff? I disabled the GPS feature, but would they keep me on the line and trace me somehow anyway? He looked at the third number he'd written down and called it.

A woman answered. "Confidential Investigations. May we help you?"

"Hi. Is . . . uh . . . the detective in? I mean—the one I saw on TV—Rachel Cord."

"I'm sorry, everyone's out on assignment at the moment. This is her answering service."

"Oh. Is there any way I can get in touch with her?"

"Are you already a client?"

"No, I'm not, but I want to hire her to find someone for me. It's pretty urgent."

"I can set up an appointment for you to see her tomorrow morning. Would ten a.m. work for you?"

"Can't I see her today? It's really important."

"I'm sure it is. I don't know when she or her associate will be back today. Why don't we make the appointment for tomorrow morning, and if either of them return or check in, I'll let them know you wish to meet sooner if possible and they can call you. May I have your name and contact number?"

"It's . . ." Do it, Terry. Do it. You have to trust someone. "Could you tell me how much she charges?"

"Her standard fee is $150 an hour with a nonrefundable $1,500 retainer up front. That covers ten hours and most expenses."

That's all? "Ah, what if she only needs an hour or two to find the person?"

"You'll have to discuss that with her. Would you like to make the appointment?"

He hesitated. Do it, already. "Okay. Yes. Yes, I would, and please be sure to let her know I want to see her today as soon as possible."

"I will. Name, please?"

"Tess . . . uh, Terry--Terry Romer."

"How do you spell that, please?"

"R-O-M-E-R."

"And Terry with a Y?"

"Yes."

"Contact number?"

He hesitated again then gave the woman his number.

"All right, Mr. Romer. If Ms. Cord or Ms. Lange return or call, I'll have them contact you. Otherwise, they'll see you tomorrow at ten. The office is in the Mann Avenue Plaza, at twelve-oh-five Mann Avenue. Do you know where that is?"

"I can google it."

"The office is in the west wing, second floor, room two-twenty-two. Thank you for calling Confidential Investigations."

Fourteen

Barbara saw Jennifer out of the corner of her eye wave at someone across the street. She looked and saw a young man in jeans, a blue long-sleeved checked shirt and black outer vest with a backpack and paper bag hurrying down the street.

"Who was that?"

"That nice guy that held the door for us at the library. Kinda cute, don't you think?"

"Hard to tell from here. But we're not here to help you find a date, remember? We had no luck at the library or the convenience store. This is our best bet. Besides, he looks too young for you."

"Spoilsport."

They went into Walgreens. The guy at the register finished ringing a purchase and bagging it for a customer.

"Thank you for choosing Walgreens. Have a nice day." He looked over at Barbara. "May I help you find something?"

"Is the manager in?"

"That's Mr. Turner. Is there a problem?"

"No. Not at all. We think one of his employees witnessed an accident and we're trying to reach her. All we have is her first name, Paula. Do you know her?"

"The only Paula that works here is Paula Fowler. She's not here now. She works the late shift. She got off at seven this morning."

"Would you know where she lives? Or her phone number?"

"I don't know her that well. You'd have to ask Mr. Turner, but we don't give out personal information."

"I understand, but this is part of an official investigation. Where may I find Mr. Turner?"

"He's either in the back checking inventory or in his office next to the pharmacy."

"Thank you."

Barbara turned and saw the pharmacy sign in the back of the store and headed that way. Jennifer followed.

"'Official investigation'? Isn't that what the cops say? Won't he think we're them?"

"Doesn't matter what he thinks. I didn't say we were cops. We were hired to find Tessa Ryker. That makes us official. That must be the office."

Paula turned over. The phone was ringing. It was way too early for anyone to call. She pulled a pillow over her head. Let voicemail get it. The ringing stopped then moments later started again. Paula continued to ignore it. It stopped and started again. Leave a message, for Crist's sake! I'm trying to sleep. The fourth time it started ringing, Paula crawled out of bed and picked up the phone.

"Hey. It's Dave at Walgreens."

"This better be important or you're dead meat. I was sound asleep."

"Sorry. The police are here looking for you."

"What?"

"I said—"

"I heard what you said. What do you mean the police are looking for me?"

"There are two of them. They must be detectives. They're not wearing uniforms. They're with Mr. Turner."

"What do they want?"

"Said you witnessed an accident and want to ask you about it."

"Accident? What accident?"

"I don't know. They didn't say. Don't you know?"

"No, I don't. Are you sure they're cops?"

"Well . . . they didn't show me badges, if that's what you mean, but they said it was official."

"Did you tell them where I live or give them my phone number?"

"Hell, no. That's private."

"What do they look like?"

"The tall one—I think she's in charge—is wearing a dark blue business suit and has her hair up. The other one is wearing a Cramer College sweatshirt and jeans. She has a ponytail. You sure you don't know what they want?"

"Not a clue. You say they're with Turner?"

"Yes. They went back to his office a couple minutes ago and I called you right away. Thought you should know."

"Thanks, Dave. I really appreciate it. I've no idea what they want. Maybe they got me mixed with someone else. Thanks, again, anyway, for the head's up."

"No problemo."

Who are they? What do they want? I doubt they're really cops. I've never witnessed an accident. That's definitely a lie. So why are they looking for me? Have I been outed somehow? That asshole almost found me once. Could he possibly —

Paula began breathing rapidly, hyperventilating and shaking.

"Get your ass back in here, woman. You hear me? Now! Don't think you can hide from me. I'll find you. You know I'll find you. And don't make me come out there after you. You won't like it if I do. I swear. You hear me?"

I hear you, asshole, but I'm not coming back. Not ever again.

"You're mine. You hear me? Mine. My wife. To honor and obey. You're mine, you stupid cunt!"

No, I'm not, asshole. I belong to me, not you.

"Come on, now. You're being foolish. You know what the Good Book says. 'We shall cleave unto each other and be one flesh.' I am your husband and you are my wife and that's the way it is. The Book says 'you will obey me.' You hear? 'The husband is the head of the wife.' It's God's will. 'You will obey your husband in everything.' Everything, you hear me? That's what it says. So stop being so damn foolish and get on back here. Now, damn it."

"Fuck you and your Good Book.

There was silence for several minutes.

"Look, darlin'. It's dark out there. Those woods are scary at night, ain't they? Can you feel it? All them bugs crawlin' about and wild animals sniffin' for prey. Hoooooowl! Come on back in here where it's safe. You belong here. You belong with me. You know you do."

No I don't. You're scarier than these woods could ever be.

"Tell you what, honey. You come back now and I won't whup you like you deserve. Okay? You know I should, but I won't do it this time. I promise. You listenin', darlin'?"

Promises. Promises. Tell that to the ER. Maybe they'll believe you like last time.

"This is 'diculous, you silly bitch. You're makin' me angry now, and you don't want to do that, now do you?"

Get as angry as you want, asshole. No fucking way I'm coming back.

"Listen. I've about had it. If you ain't back in this house in five minutes, I'm gonna feed that stupid cat of yours to Butch then send him out to get you. You hear me? I said, 'You hear me?' Answer me, you fucking cunt."

She felt the large lump in her shoulder bag squirm. "It's okay, Pumpkin," she whispered. "Butch isn't going to eat you or find me. Not tonight, anyway. Maybe never after what I gave him for supper. Let's go. It's time to get out of here."

Tears welled in her eyes as Paula remembered Pumpkin Patch, the white cat with orange spots she'd found abandoned as a kitten. I miss you, baby. Hope you're happy. Those kind ladies said they'd find you a good home. I couldn't take you with me. Sorry. She wiped the tears from her eyes.

Slowly, she began breathing normally again. Calmer. Maybe this isn't about me. Maybe I'm overreacting. Anonymity is too good. That me is long dead and buried. Whatever these women want from me, it can't have anything to do with him. And they won't find me through Turner. He's too much the rule follower.

"I'm not supposed to give out employees home addresses."

"We appreciate that, Mr. Turner."

"And Ms. Fowler is an excellent worker." Turner tapped the open file on the desk. "She's been with us several years. I can't believe she's done anything wrong."

"As I said, Mr. Turner, she hasn't done anything wrong. Another witness to the accident described her to us, and that description we've discovered matches Paula Fowler. We just want to meet her and verify what she saw that day."

"Sorry. I can't let you have that information. You'll have to come back when she's working."

"Does she work tonight?"

"Yes. Her shift starts at eleven."

"Thank you, Mr. Turner, for seeing us. We understand your position. We'll be back tonight."

"Sorry, but rules are rules."

"Of course they are. Thank you, again. Good-bye."

As they left Walgreens, Barbara pulled her iPad out of her bag and turned it on.

"That was a waste of time. Oh, great."

"What?"

"I've got a dozen text messages from Rachel and a slew of voicemail. Want to bet those are from her too?"

"No bets."

"I can't blow her off, but I thought we'd have a solid lead by now. I'll try LexisNexis to locate Fowler. If that doesn't work, I'll have to call Rachel."

"Why don't we just go to the Radford Park Apartments, 1595 Radford Avenue, Building 7, Apartment C-6, instead?"

"How'd you get that?"

"Turner had Fowler's file open on his desk. I can read upside down writing. While you two talked, I read the top sheet."

Ten minutes later Barbara rang the bell to Paula Fowler's apartment. A moment later she saw the peephole go dark.

"Who is it?"

"I'm Barbara Lange and my associate is Jennifer Hackett. May we speak with you, Ms. Fowler?"

"Are you the two that were looking for me at Walgreens?"

Barbara and Jennifer looked at each other. Jennifer shrugged.

"Yes we are," Barbara said.

"Well I don't know anything about any accident, so go away."

"That's true, you don't. I'm sorry. That was a subterfuge I used as I didn't want your boss to know the real reason we need to speak with you."

"Yeah, well, it pisses me off and I have no need to talk to you. Did Turner give you this address? Because if he did—"

"No, he didn't. We found it on our own. Would you open the door, please? It's very difficult trying to talk through it."

"Not my problem. What makes you think I'll talk to you after you lied to find me?"

"Ms. Fowler, we're trying to find a girl that—"

"If you want a girl, try Phil's Tearoom in South Ferry. That's where all the lezzies hang out."

"Would you please—"

"Go away or I'll call the cops. The *real* cops. Let 'em know you were impersonating them."

"We did not—"

"Ms. Fowler? This is Jennifer Hackett. We did not impersonate police officers. You can verify that with Mr. Turner. If anyone told you otherwise, they are mistaken. We're very sorry for the subterfuge."

"You mean lies."

"Yes, you're correct, I mean lies. We truly apologize for that. We work for a private detective agency. Barb, show her your ID." Barbara held her investigator's license up to the peephole. "We've been hired to find a runaway girl. You were seen having breakfast with someone who resembles her two weeks ago at Belle's Diner. Please let us in. We just want to know what you can tell us about that girl. Please. She needs to be found. She's alone. Probably scared. She's only fourteen. We want to help her."

There was no reply. Jennifer and Barbara were afraid they missed out again when they heard the latch unlock and the door open.

Paula reached out her hand. "Let me see your license."

Barbara handed it to her. She examined it and handed it back. She turned to Jennifer.

"Let me see yours."

"I'm afraid I don't have one. I only work for the agency part time in the office. I haven't applied for a state investigator license yet. All I have is my driver's license, if you want to see that."

Paula shook her head. "Come on in."

The apartment was small but tidy; the furniture thrift store chic. There were two comfortable armchairs, two floor lamps, a large futon for a couch, a glass-topped coffee table and across the room a 32-inch flat screen television on a low bookcase filled with a DVD player, DVDs and several paperbacks. The room was open to the kitchen and a small dinette table with two chairs was against the large window that overlooked Radford Park. Three doors that indicated bedroom, bath and closet were all closed.

"You might as well sit down. Now, what's this about a girl?"

"We're looking for this girl." Barbara took out the picture of Tessa Ryker.

Paula rose. "I get it. That's the girl on TV. The one that supposedly killed her family. You're lousy bounty hunters. Out for the reward. I've never seen her. Get out of here."

Barbara and Jennifer stood leaving the photograph on the coffee table.

"We're not bounty hunters. We're—"

"Please leave my home."

"Ms. Fowler—"

"I said, 'please leave', or I *will* call the cops."

"Ms. Fowler, Barbara's correct. We aren't bounty hunters. We're not out for the reward money. We're very concerned for Tessa Ryker's wellbeing. We don't believe she killed anyone, least of all her family. She may be running from the real killer for all we know. You met her. Had breakfast with her. Talked with her. Please help us."

Paula looked at both of them, deciding. She turned to Barbara.

"I don't like you. You can wait outside. I'll talk to her."

Barbara left and Jennifer sat back down taking a slim notepad from her pocket. Paula sat across from her.

"You're wrong. I've never met that girl."

"Are you sure? This is an old picture. You did have breakfast two weeks ago, October ninth, at Belle's, with someone who looks a lot like her, didn't you?"

"Yes, I did, but I'm positive it wasn't this girl. The girl I was with was older. Sixteen, I think, at least."

"What can you tell me about her?"

"Not much, really. I bought her breakfast is all. Haven't seen her since. Definitely not Ryker, though."

"How did you meet?"

"At Walgreens. She wandered in about five looking lost. Thought she was a runaway. I watched her to be sure she didn't steal anything. I'm alone there at night right now. I've told Turner, he's the manager you know, we need a second person at night but he hasn't hired one yet."

"How did you end up at breakfast with her?"

"Well, after she wandered about a bit, she finally bought a candy bar. She had to go through all her pockets to find enough change. I asked if she were hungry and offered to buy her breakfast at Belle's. Told her where it was and that I'd meet her there right after I got off at seven."

"Did she talk much?

"Not a whole lot. She was real hungry though. Ate two of Belle's waffles and they're pretty filling."

"I know. I had one earlier. Did she say where she was from? Have a name?"

Paula paused, thinking. She glanced about then looked straight at Jennifer.

"Just her first name. Cindy Lou. That was it. Cindy Lou. Said she was from Little Rock, but I doubt it. Her accent was strong. I'd say south Louisiana. Cajun country definitely. That's another reason I'm sure she couldn't have been the Ryker girl."

Jennifer nodded. "Did she say why she ran away?"

"The usual. Parents didn't understand her."

"Did you bring her here?"

"No. We parted right after breakfast. I didn't think she had any money so I gave her $60. All I had on me."

"That was very generous."

"I sympathized with her. I ran away once too. People helped me then. Just thought of it as paying it forward."

"Do you know where she went after you parted?"

"No. She walked . . . I think south—yes, definitely south— on Twenty-First Street and I came home."

Jennifer couldn't think of another question and rose. "Well, thank you for seeing us. Oh, one last thing. I understand your cousin is staying with you."

"Who told you that?"

"One of the waitresses at Belle's."

"Hmmm. What about him?"

"Any chance he saw or met the girl?"

"I highly doubt it. Terry didn't get here until the next day."

"All right. Thanks again. I'm really sorry for any misunderstanding."

"Apology accepted."

Jennifer joined Barbara at the car.

"Anything?"

Jennifer shook her head. "Not really. Were you upset she kicked you out?"

"It happens. She took to you though. That's all that counts. What's important is did she know anything?"

"That's hard to say. She kept saying it wasn't Tessa. Emphasized it. Said the girl was older and had a strong Cajun accent."

"Did you believe her?"

"That's the hard part. I'm not as experienced interviewing people as you and Rachel are. Maybe she sensed that and that's why she talked with me and not you. Some of her answers were glib and quick—almost as if practiced. While other times she hesitated before answering like she was making it up on the spot. Whether she lied or told the truth, I can't be certain. Sorry."

"What's your gut feeling?"

"That she's hiding something. I don't know what though."

"Okay. She'll need some more looking at."

"What next?"

"Back to the office. Not all my voicemails were from Rachel. Some were people calling in with negative reports on sighting Tessa, but Angie over at Paying It Forward gave me a possible lead I want to check out."

"'Paying it forward'? Paula mentioned that."

"What do you mean?"

She said she gave the girl $60, which I thought pretty generous, and she said she did it because people helped her once so she considered this 'paying it forward.'"

"'Paying it forward' is an age-old principle. Help someone because someone else helped you. Ben Franklin practiced it. Angie's group is dedicated to following it. Still, it's interesting that Paula used that phrase. I wonder . . .?"

"What?"

"I spoke with Angie while waiting for you. She said a couple of her volunteers dropped out. They didn't think the group went far enough to help people. Especially those escaping dangerous situations. She thought they might have joined Anonymity, an organization I've never heard of."

"Isn't that that hacker group that attacks governments and corporations? You know, the ones with the Guy Fawkes masks."

"You're thinking of Anonymous. But Anonymity is nearly as radical according to Angie. She says they'll go to any length to help someone hide. Even illegal ones. She doesn't know much about the group, just that it's pretty secret and dedicated to people who need to disappear. Let me see if Paula was one of her dropouts."

The call went directly to voicemail.

"Angie? This is Barb. I've got a couple questions about those volunteers of yours that left. Please call me back soonest. Thanks." Barbara hung up and shrugged. "Let's go see how mad Rachel is."

Fifteen

Terry went back to the library but didn't stay long. He was too nervous about the ammunition and gun clips in his backpack and kept hoping his phone would ring. He had no real plan, just needed to find the sheriff. Find him. Make him confess. Or kill him.

Searching the Internet was no help. There was nothing new on his family's murders or the search for him—her. Nothing told him where to find the sheriff. Frustrated he packed his laptop and got up to leave. Carrie and Christine had been watching him. Carrie asked if he were all right. Said he looked worried.

"I'm fine, ma'am," he reassured her. "Just trying to decide what to do with my life."

"You're young," Christine said. "You've got lots of time to figure that out."

"Yes, ma'am. Thank you. See you ladies tomorrow."

He walked across the street to the convenience store. Bought a soda and an apple fritter then sat on a bench outside. He checked his phone to be sure it was on and put it back in his pocket. When he finished his snack he headed for home. Paula should still be asleep. He'd have time to hide the ammunition and clips in the closet. If only one of those detectives would call.

As Terry neared the entrance to the apartment complex, he saw a red sports car leave the parking lot and drive past him. He turned to look at it. Where'd I see that car before? He shook his head. He was sure he'd seen it but couldn't quite place it. It wasn't at the apartments. Was it the library? Probably not important. He headed across the parking lot to Paula's apartment. At the foot of the stairs his phone rang. He dropped it trying to get it out of his pocket too fast. He picked it up and flipped it open.

"Hello?"

"Is this Terry Romer?"

He hesitated. "Yes, it is."

"This is Rachel Cord. My answering service said you needed to speak with me urgently."

Terry sighed with relief. "Yes, ma'am. Thank you for calling. I need to hire you. I need to find someone right away. It's really important. *Extremely* important. Can I hire you right away?"

"We're in the middle of something at the moment. You have an appointment to see me in the morning. Can't this wait until then?"

"I *really* need to find this man. The sooner the better. *Today*, if possible. I know what you charge. I can pay you."

"Who is he?"

"He's . . ." What do I say? He killed my family? He's the sheriff? What?

"Are you still there?"

"Yes. Yes. I . . . I'm not sure what to say. On the phone. Can't I see you right away? Please. Please."

There was a pause. "I can see you at three o'clock. Will that work?"

Terry glanced at the time on his phone: 11:30.

"Yes. Yes. Thank you."

"Do you have my address or should I come to you?"

Terry looked up at Paula's door. "Your office. I'll be there. Thank you. Thank you *so* much."

He closed the phone and clutched it to his chest. Took several deep breaths. I'm going to find you, Sheriff Donahue. I'm going to get you. He opened the phone, turned it off, put it in his pocket and climbed the stairs to Paula's apartment.

Terry was surprised to see Paula standing by the dinette table staring out at the park. Paula turned quickly.

"Thank God, you're back."

"What happened? Why aren't you asleep?"

"We need to get you away from here. Now."

"Why? What happened?"

"Two people were just here looking for you. Looking for Tessa."

"What? How?"

"They found out I had breakfast with you—with Tessa—two weeks ago."

"How?"

"I don't know how but they did. We have to get you out of here. You're not safe here any longer."

"What did you tell them?"

"I lied. I think they're after the reward for you. I said it wasn't you I had breakfast with. Made up a name. Said you were from Louisiana. Cajun. The first thing I could think of. Never saw you again after that morning."

"Did they believe you?"

"I think so, but that's not the point. People have connected us. You're not safe here."

Terry thought of his appointment with the detective.

"I can't leave yet."

"You have to. Don't you understand? Your new identity is only good if no one connects it to Tessa. We can't take chances. Believe me, I know. You have to leave."

"I do understand but there are things I have to do today. Today, Paula. Here. Please understand how important this is for me."

"Let me think."

Shaking her head, Paula went to the sink and drank some water as Terry watched her. She stood there for several moments with her eyes closed shaking her head. She turned around.

"Okay. I have a friend in Chester you can stay with a few days. She's totally trustworthy and won't ask questions. You need to leave here. You really do. Trust me on that."

"Where's Chester?"

"West of here. About thirty minutes. Pack and I'll take you."

"I need to be somewhere at three o'clock."

"Tessa."

"I'm Terry. Terry Romer. Thanks to you and Anonymity, I know. And I appreciate it. I do. But I have to do this first. I have to. I'll pack. Get ready. But you can take me to your friend's later—this evening—before work. I'll be back in plenty of time. I promise."

Paula shook her head. "It's dangerous waiting, even a few hours, but all right if it's that important. You promise?"

"Cross my heart. I'll pack my things now. Why don't you go back to bed?"

"Too wired. I'll shower and then call Pete."

"Pete?"

Paula smiled. "My friend's nickname. Her real name is Patricia, but she's been Pete since birth. The story she tells is her parents at one point thought they were having twins or possibly even triplets. They jokingly called them Pete, Repeat and Little Dorothy. Her brother, who was two, kept asking 'When's Pete coming?' and started calling her that when she was born."

Terry smiled at Paula's attempt to ease the tension. Paula went to her bedroom and closed the door. Terry waited and listened. He heard her go into the bathroom from the bedroom side, lock the door to the living room and start the shower.

He pulled his duffel from the hall closet. He took the paper bag with the ammunition and clips from his backpack and loaded both clips. He stuffed the extra ammo in the bottom of his duffel and took out another $5,000 that he put in his backpack. He took out the gun and the baggie with the original clip and bullet. He put the baggie in his backpack. He loaded the gun and put it and the extra clip in his backpack. He packed the rest of his clothes from the closet into the duffel, closed it and put it on the futon.

Terry looked at the bathroom door and heaved a big sigh. He had three hours before seeing the detective but didn't want to wait here and have Paula try to talk him into leaving for her friend's house right away. He picked up his backpack. He wasn't sure he was doing the right thing, but it was what he had to do. He gave the bathroom door a final glance.

I promise, Paula, I'll be back if I can. If not, thanks for everything.

Sixteen

I stared at my phone. There was something odd about the person I'd just spoken with. I walked down the hall to the reception area.

"Doris? You took that call from Terry Romer, didn't you?"

"Yes. Why?"

"How did he sound to you?"

"Anxious, maybe? And pleading but not whiny. He really wanted to see you right away."

"How old would you say he is?"

"I don't know. He had a nice voice. He seemed nervous though. I'd say early twenties, maybe. Possibly slightly younger. It's hard to tell on the phone sometimes. Are you meeting him today?"

"Yes. Three o'clock. When you spoke with him, were you sure you were speaking to a guy?"

"Definitely. Why? Do you think he's a she?"

"I can't put my finger on it. I thought I was talking with an adult male, but for a moment, something he said or the way he said it, made me think otherwise. Not important. I'll know at three. Have you heard anything from Barbara?"

"Not a word."

"Thanks."

I went back to my office. I had Tessa Ryker's belongings laid out on the school desks. I'd checked them twice finding nothing. I put vinyl gloves back on and used a magnifying glass to see if I missed anything of value. Nothing gave me the slightest clue as to where she was now or what she looked like. Maybe the police lab would have better luck when I turned all this over to Wainwright.

I went back to my desk and reread the draft report Barb started. I made a few changes and additions, but, basically, we had very little new for Sheriff Donahue. Nothing that proved she was still in town or where she might have gone. I heard the other office door open and looked up. Barbara appeared in the entry to my office.

"Hi." She sounded sheepish and uncomfortable. As well she should.

"Where you been?"

She came into the room.

"Tracking down a lead."

"And you couldn't leave me a message or call to let me know or turn your phone on so I could reach you?"

Jennifer appeared in the doorway with a box of donuts.

"That was my fault."

"Really? Thought you were working at MGT today."

"I took the day off to help Barb. What's all that?"

"Tessa Ryker's belongings. They were dropped in a Salvation Army bin out at Westbrook Mall sometime last week." I looked at Barb. "Your friend, Teri Underwood, called this morning and I went and picked them up."

"Teri's good."

"Yes, she is. I didn't find anything there that would help us though. I even went out to the mall and went through a week of their security videos. No sign of Tessa or who dropped her stuff off. Now let's get back to where you two have been." I stood. "I see you brought sweets to calm the savage beast. There's fresh coffee. We might as well get comfortable. I'm sure you have an interesting story to tell me."

I went and sat on one of the loveseats by the windows. It's always been one of my favorite thinking spots and gets great views of sunsets and storms. Jen laid the donut box on the coffee table and opened it then sat opposite me as Barb fetched coffee for all of us. Jen knew my weakness and half the box was a variety of chocolate donuts. I picked out a glazed chocolate cake one and waited for Barb to sit. They both seemed nervous. I waited to see who would start.

"Jen found—" "Tessa posted—"

"Stop. One at a time, please.

"We stayed late. Jen was going through all the data she'd downloaded and I was working on background checks. I finished several."

"I know. Mary told me when I came in and I saw the copies you left me. Go on."

"Anyway, Jen found a reply to a tweet on one of Tessa's friends' Twitter accounts that she thought was from Tessa."

"Whose account?"

"Hildred Speaks," Jen said. "She wasn't on the list the sheriff gave us. She's one of the ones I added. Her Twitter name is *HildySpeaksTrue*. She tweeted on the ninth that someone said there was proof Tessa killed her family. Tessa replied it was a lie the next day."

"How did you know it was Tessa? Did she use her own Twitter login?"

"No. Tessa's Twitter name is *Whim-me*. That account's still dormant. She used her mom's. I doubt anyone but Tessa would have known her mom's login password."

"Do you know who said there was proof of her guilt?"

"Tommy Wagner, another friend and the son of the sheriff's chief deputy, Harold Wagner."

"That's not what Donahue told us."

"I know. I think Wagner let it slip out at home and Tommy repeated it."

"That bothers me we weren't told that, if it's true. Nor was it in the file Donahue gave us. I'll have to ask him about it when he gets here this afternoon. Did you notify Detective

Anderson or her partner about the tweet so they could track down the source?"

They looked at each other and Barb shook her head.

"No, we didn't. We thought we'd check it out first to be sure it was from Tessa."

"How did you do that?"

"Jen traced where the reply originated." Barb's voice got very quiet.

I looked at Jen. "Do I want to know how you did that? Never mind. Rhetorical question. What did you find out?"

They told me about tracing it to the Hanson memorial library but striking out at the library and nearby convenience store on Tessa sightings. They did catch a hot lead at Belle's Diner however.

I remembered Belle's. Hadn't been there in a few years. Went pretty often for a while. Have to go back. They had great old-fashioned, thick milkshakes made with real ice cream and wonderfully crisp fries and onion rings. They even had a vegan burger for Wendy. Wonder if I know any of the current staff.

"Anyway, that led us to Walgreens where we got Paula Fowler's full name and address and went to interview her."

They described the difficulties they had getting her to talk to them. I found it amusing Barb getting kicked out and Jen doing the interview.

"Who do you think warned her you were coming?"

"The clerk at the counter. He had enough time while we spoke to the manager, and Fowler thought we were impersonating the police. The manager knew better."

Jen pulled out her notepad and described her interview with Fowler.

"How much of what Fowler said do you think is true?"

"Fifty-fifty. I think what she said about how they met and taking her to breakfast is accurate. I think she made up the parts of the girl not being Tessa. Let's face it, a Cajun named Cindy Lou is hard to swallow."

"Cindy Lou who?"

"Damn!" Barb exclaimed. We looked at her. "I just got it. Cindy Lou Who. Come on. You both know her. *Cindy Lou Who? Dr. Seuss? How the Grinch Stole Christmas?* Fowler was playing us the whole time. I bet she made that stink to get rid of me because she thought you'd be easier to lie to, Jen. Cindy Lou was probably the first name she could think up."

Jen nodded. "She did pause a long time before giving me the name. I thought she was trying to remember it. And she was staring at the television set."

I smiled. "What does that tell us?"

"That the girl she was with *was* Tessa Ryker."

"And," Jen added, "that they probably didn't separate after leaving Belle's. I'm betting she took her home with her which means Fowler's cousin Terry probably met her too. He's probably been helping Fowler hide her."

"Another Terry? We seem to be wading in Terrys all of a sudden."

"How so?"

"First: Terry Ryker, the father. Then Teri Underwood at Salvation Army. Now your Terry, Paula Fowler's cousin. Finally, there's Terry Romer, my three o'clock appointment."

"Who's he?"

"I'm not sure. He called while we were out this morning but wants to see me ASAP. I spoke to him a bit ago. Wants us to find someone right away. Seems to think we can do it instantly."

Barb stood. "That'd be novel. Anyone want more coffee?"

Jen nodded and passed Barb her cup as she grabbed another donut. I stood also.

"No, thanks. We need to finish the report for Donahue. He's meeting us here at one-thirty."

"Rachel?"

"Yes, Jen?"

She hesitated. "Do we have to put everything in the report?"

"If you're worried about him knowing how you tracked Tessa's tweet, I'm not going to include that."

"It's not that. It's . . ."

"What?"

"I don't trust the sheriff."

"Why not?"

"She said the same thing to me last night," Barb said returning with the coffee.

"I'm listening."

Jen took a bite of her donut. Barb and I sat back down and waited.

"It's hard to explain. The sheriff hired you and is paying you privately. I don't understand that. Wait. That's not where I want to start. Okay. Tessa Ryker's phone GPS put her in the area when the murders occurred. Right?"

"Yes."

"She took clothes, money, her mom's credit card and her dad's truck and fled shortly later. She drove here and disappeared."

"That's right."

"So she must have seen her family's bodies, but she made no attempt to contact the sheriff's department. She just ran away."

"True."

"Why?"

"That's the big question, and we won't get an answer unless we find her."

"And she hasn't contacted any other police agency."

"Not that we know of. What's your point?"

Jen took a deep breath. "I think Tessa's too scared to go to the police because she's afraid they will let the killer know where she is."

"What? Why would she think that?"

"Because she saw the killer. I don't think she was in the house. Nearby though. She played hooky from school that day. Maybe she heard the shots. I don't know, but I think she must have seen the killer leaving at the very least and recognized him."

"You're assuming she didn't kill her family."

"True. I am. She claims in her tweet to Hildy she didn't do it. I believe her. Why would she kill her parents? Her little sister? Where would she get the gun to do it? They didn't own guns. Hadn't for years. The killer must have brought it. The killer she recognized and is afraid of." Jen took another breath. "I think the sheriff killed her family. I don't know why, but that's why she won't go to the police. I think he realizes that and that's why he hired you to find her."

"You seriously think he did it?"

"Yes, I do. I don't think he cares for her like he claims. It made no sense to me he'd hire you. He's the Law. Every other law agency is helping him. Why does he need you?"

I looked at Barb and she shrugged.

"It does answer some questions. I sorta suggested the same thing yesterday but didn't consider Sheriff Donahue as who she saw."

They looked at me but stayed quiet letting me digest the possibilities. Over the years I've cooperated with the law numerous times, but being hired by a law officer was uniquely unusual. That's not quite true. Det. Wayne Jablowski hired me once to find his foster daughter who'd run away. So was this that far out? If Jen was right—and Barb was leaning that way too—and we found Tessa Ryker, we could be leading her family's killer right to her.

Was I wrong to trust Donahue? I'd liked him right off. He was recommended by someone I trust, but was that enough to take him at face value. Was I taken in by his cool voice, looks and laid-back, self-deprecating manner? I got up and went to my desk. I opened the file folder he'd given us. There was a lot of information there. Was it too much? Was it just the facts or was it smokescreen to hide a personal agenda?

I looked at the schoolhouse clock above the blackboard. 12:15. Donahue was due here at 1:30. That didn't leave much time to decide what to tell him.

"We have less than an hour to finish the report. Donahue strikes me as the come early type. Barb. Call Detective Anderson or Kern. Tell them about the tweet and that you suspect it came from Tessa. Don't mention we traced it. Also include your interviews at Belle's—say we got an anonymous tip—but leave out IDing Fowler and her interview for now and tell them about finding Tessa's stuff. Then try to get them to open up about their investigation. I've found that giving often gets in return. Maybe we can glean something new from them. Jen. Run a quick background on Paula Fowler. Let's see who she is. Do we know her cousin's full name?

"No. Just that he's from Colorado. Golden or Boulder."

"Okay. If a Terry in Colorado shows up in her report, assume it's him and check that too. I'll start massaging our report."

As I sat at my computer Barb came over.

"There's another wrinkle we should look at."

"What's that?

Angie from Paying It Forward told me there's a radical and somewhat secret group called Anonymity that helps victims of domestic and sexual abuse. She said a couple of her volunteers quit and may have joined it. I'm waiting for her to call back to see if Fowler was one of those volunteers. I also wanted to see what I could find on the group online."

"How radical?"

"Angie didn't know much but said they go to extreme lengths to hide and protect victims. If Fowler is connected with them, they could be hiding Tessa and why she's off everyone's radar."

"Possibly. Talk to the sheriff's detectives first. If Angie hasn't called back by then, call her again. Then I want you to go over this report with me before Donahue gets here. Checking that group will have to wait until later."

Lying to a client is not good business. Nor was leading a killer to his victim. That was my problem. Which was Sheriff Donahue? Concerned friend and law officer or cold-blooded killer? Have I ever had a similar situation?

I suppose I should include Warren Daniels. He was an uncomfortable surprise. If Raines hadn't been in the office yesterday, would Daniels have gone across the river and shot both his wife and cousin in their pied-à-terre? Probably not. He was more upset about the embezzling than the adultery.

There was Stanley Kay. When was that? It was early on. I'd been open . . . two years? Three? No. Nearly two. December '99. His wife hired me to find him. I found out two days in that he was a battered husband and hiding from her. I returned her retainer and warned him she might hire a different agency to locate him.

Enough woolgathering. That doesn't solve this problem. I opened the draft report. I put in most of what we had done leaving out only the tracing of the tweet and Fowler's identity and interview. Between the three of us, we had more than used up Donahue's retainer and could justify waiting to see if he wanted us to pursue leads or not.

Jen came over. "Here's what I've got on Fowler. She's twenty-six. I thought she was younger. Paula Anne Fowler, born Santa Rosa, California, August first, nineteen-ninety-three. Parents deceased. No siblings. High school graduate. Two years at Humboldt State University. No degree."

"Where's that?"

"Northern California. She's lived in Douglas, Arizona, Midland, Texas, and Shreveport, Louisiana, before coming here three years ago. No criminal record. The only Terry that came up as a possible associate is a forty-year-old woman currently living in Grants, New Mexico. Apparently they had the same address in Douglas."

"Could be coincidence. Whether they were at that address at the same time or not is questionable. These background searches often make associations that aren't accurate and have to be checked out further. We don't have the time or need at the moment. Thanks. Here. Take a look at what I've written and see if I've left anything in we don't want revealed or been too vague."

Jen sped through the report then went back through it again more slowly.

"Looks okay to me, but won't the sheriff wonder why we didn't try to find Fowler?"

"My plan is to tell him he only paid for ten hours and we've exceeded that. We'll gladly continue and try to locate that unknown woman at the diner if he wants, but it's his decision to make. If he's legitimate, I expect him to say, 'Thanks,' and turn everything over to the local authorities to look into. On the other hand—"

Barb came in shaking her head. "Angie doesn't know Fowler. She's not one of the volunteers that quit. That's a bust. I spoke with Detective Anderson and she appreciated the tip on the tweet. She hadn't seen it but was going to check it out right away. She's really pissed that Chief Deputy Wagner would say something like that to his family, as she says it isn't true. And—more as an aside—she said she doesn't understand why he's so adamant about that theory. From the way she talked, I think she was already pissed with him about the investigation. She muttered something about him always fucking it up. I think an earthquake's coming to downtown Hartfield this afternoon."

"Glad we could help."

"Oh, and you were right. She did share some information."

"What?"

"She said some of the evidence bothered her, and because of it, she believes someone tried to make it look like Ryker killed his family. And she doesn't think Tessa could have done it."

"What evidence?"

Barb opened the file folder Donahue gave us and began flipping through it.

"Two things. First, the shot that was fired into the living room wall and presumed to have missed Mrs. Ryker as she was fleeing."

Barb turned the folder toward us and pointed to a photograph.

"This is it. What's not in this report is that according to the forensic team that bullet couldn't have been fired from a standing position while the two bullets that struck her were. The angle of trajectory is totally wrong. That bullet was fired from a low angle near the floor where Ryker was laying. Which makes no sense if Ryker shot his wife before killing himself and definitely couldn't after."

Barb flipped the folder to two photos showing Ryker's hands.

"The second thing the team found confusing has to do with the GSR and blood splatter on Ryker's hands. There is splatter—more like a mist according to Anderson—and GSR on both hands. She said the blood splatter and GSR on the right hand were contemporaneous—not sure what that means—whereas on the left hand there was a slight smearing and additional GSR on top of the smears. I hope I'm explaining this right."

"You're doing fine. Go on."

"Okay. The only way Anderson believes these facts can be explained is that Ryker must have struggled with his killer—whoever that is—and was holding the gun by the barrel with both hands when it went off striking him beneath the chin. Then the killer immediately shot Mrs. Ryker as she ran from the room. The little girl, Katrina, who was home ill, must have heard the shots and come out of her room. The killer then shot her too. Anderson says the killer then put the gun in Ryker's left hand and fired the shot at the wall so it would appear Ryker fired the gun and thus cover up the crime. She doesn't believe Tessa has the sophistication or knowledge to do that."

"I take it Ryker was left-handed?"

"Yes. Anderson said that's pretty common knowledge. However, she said what's less known is that Ryker was right-eye dominant and always fired rifles and pistols right-handed. That's something Tessa would know, and the killer either didn't know or forgot in the heat of the moment."

"What's GSR?"

I turned to Jen. "Gunshot residue. When any gun is fired, gases and bits of unburned primer and gunpowder are expelled along with the bullet and not necessarily all out the end of the barrel. It will be on the shooter's gun hand or hands if he used a two-hand grip, possibly his clothes and objects nearby. For example, if I fired a pistol sitting here, GSR might be on my computer helping establish where I fired from. Also GSR will be on the victim if he was close enough like on Ryker but not on his wife. The killer made serious mistakes trying to be clever."

Barb closed the file folder. "The sheriff says he's known Ryker since high school. Would he have made that kind of mistake about the hand?"

"I don't know. When you've just murdered three people, people who were your friends and one a young girl, you're not going to be thinking straight. You're panicky. Could happen. This is good information but doesn't give us answers about Donahue or where Tessa is." I turned my computer around. "Read the report and tell me what you think."

Barb read it through three times and made two minor suggestions. We incorporated those, made a back-up copy and sent the document to print. Barb assembled the report in a nice folder and Jen made fresh coffee. I glanced at the clock. Twenty minutes before Donahue was due if he wasn't early. I needed to make another decision.

"Thank you, ladies. You've done great work. Why don't you go have a nice lunch on me."

Barb handed me the report. "Now? With the sheriff coming? You trying to get rid of us?"

"Yeah," said Jen. "Shouldn't we stay and help brief him?"

"That's not necessary. Everything we want him to know is in the report and I can easily go over it with him. It doesn't need three of us. Besides, I thought I'd treat the two of you. You put in a long night and morning."

"What's the real reason, Rachel? Don't trust us? Afraid Jen or I will say or do something to give our suspicions away?"

"Trust you? Absolutely. Afraid? In a way, yes. If we're all here, and he asks a question we'd rather avoid, I'm afraid we'd all try to say something at the same time and possibly contradictory. I think it would be simpler and less likely to arouse his suspicions for just one of us to brief him. As the boss, that means me."

"I recognize the risk, but—"

There was a knock and the door to the outer office opened.

"Hello? Anyone here? It's Sheriff Donahue."

"Looks like this discussion's moot." I stood and came around my desk. "In here, Sheriff."

Seventeen

The sheriff came in and glanced around. The schoolroom look of my private office can seem strange to some, but he didn't seem bothered by it.

"I'm a bit early. Habit of mine. Hope I'm not interrupting something. I can wait in the other room."

"Not a problem. We were just going over your report. You met Barbara yesterday; this is Jennifer Hackett. She helps us part-time with computer research."

"Baxter Donahue. Pleased to meet you."

He held out his hand and Jen hesitated slightly before taking it and smiling.

"Jennifer or Jen. Pleased to meet you, too."

"Computer research? Are you the one that caught that tweet to Hildy Speaks?"

Jen's eyes flickered at me before answering. "Yes. How do you know about it?"

"Had a call from Debra, Detective Anderson, on my way here. She told me about Ms. Lange's call. That was a good catch." He smiled taking us all in. "She also ripped my ear off complaining about my chief deputy's big mouth. Knowing her, though, I'm sure she laid into him even worse than she did me."

I stepped forward. "So is there positive evidence or not about Tessa's guilt? You didn't indicate that yesterday."

"I believe I said that Harry and Wade Vanderhorn are pushing that line of thought. And no, the evidence isn't there. I agree with Debra the evidence points away from Tessa's involvement." He shook his head. "I've had problems with Harry like this other times too. I keep telling him, 'you have to go with the evidence as it is, not what you want it to be.' Guess he and I are going to have to have another talk. If Debra's left any of him alive, that is."

He gave another of his Sam Elliot smiles with a twinkle in his eye then looked at the things spread on the student tables.

"That Tessa's stuff?"

"Yes, it is. I picked it up this morning from Salvation Army. It was put in one of their bins last week out at Westbrook Mall. I spent a good portion of the morning going through the mall security footage. Didn't see who dropped the stuff off or anyone who looked like Ryker."

He walked over to the tables and looked closely at the clothes and shoes but didn't touch anything.

"So she's got new duds. Probably changed her hair too. Dyed it, maybe."

"A distinct possibility. I didn't find anything to indicate what she looks like now or where she's been staying."

"Curious."

"What?"

"Terry's duffel bag. This looks like everything we think Tessa took with her. It would all fit in that sports bag there. Why would she need her dad's duffel too? Was something else in it?"

"No idea. It's completely empty."

"What are you going to do with it?"

"Take it to Sergeant Wainwright later. Maybe their lab can find some trace evidence that'll be useful."

"I can drop it off. I'm seeing him after I leave here."

"Okay. Jen. Would you pack everything back into the sports bag, please? Put it in that trash bag and use gloves so you don't contaminate anything any more than the Salvation

Army people already have. Sheriff, why don't we sit and be comfortable? Would you like some coffee? It's freshly made."

I picked up his report and we walked over to the loveseats and sat.

"No, thank you. I had lunch just before coming here at that place you recommended. Great little restaurant. Thank you." He looked up at Barb. "Ms. Lange, Barbara. Deb—Detective Anderson says you interviewed some people that saw Tessa at a diner."

Barb sat beside me. "That's right. A waitress and a customer. A regular who's there most mornings. This was very early on the ninth a little before six. The diner opens at five-thirty. She came in and had breakfast. Their description of her matched the way she looked earlier at the bus station except she had added a baseball cap to hide her hair."

"And there was a woman with her?"

"Yes. Not at first. They said the woman joined her later and ate also. Neither of the witnesses knew who the woman was though. They left together, but no one saw which way they went."

"About the cap. Did your witnesses say what color it was or if it had a logo?"

"It was a red Cardinals' cap."

"Hmm. Terry favored the Twins and Caroline liked the Mariners. Both owned caps and jackets. Tessa must have picked this one up here. Was the cap new?"

"Witnesses didn't say."

He nodded, hunched over, looking down at the coffee table, thinking, and then straightened up.

"Did the woman just come in and sit with Tessa or did she talk to her first like introducing herself?"

"Neither witness mentioned that, and I didn't think to ask. Sorry."

"It's all right. They may not have remembered anyway. Who paid for breakfast?

"The woman did. Paid cash."

"And they left together?"

"Yes."

"Had any luck locating this woman?"

I leaned forward. "Barb only interviewed the witnesses this morning. There hasn't been time for follow-ups. We can do that—we have a good description of the woman to work with—but between yesterday and today, we've put in more hours than your retainer covered."

"So I owe you some and you need more to continue?"

"'Fraid so. Of course you can take what we've gotten so far to Sergeant Wainwright to pursue. It's all in this report."

I handed him the folder. He sat back and opened it. He took a glasses case from his coat and put on a pair of wire-rimmed half-glasses and began reading.

"Sure you don't want some coffee?"

"No, I'm good. Thanks."

As he read, he'd glance up at me or Barb or over at Jen, who had finished packing Tessa's stuff and was sitting at one of the student tables with a cup of coffee and a donut. He flipped back a couple pages.

"I don't see a name for the person that called in the tip about the diner."

"Jen took the call. The caller asked for Barb, but she was down the hall at the time. He didn't give his name and Jen didn't recognize his voice. All he said was he might have seen the missing girl go in the diner a couple weeks ago. Barb checked it out and verified it. She also checked at the library across the street and the convenience store next door to see if Tessa stayed in the area. No one remembers seeing her."

He nodded and continued reading. He spent some time studying the last page that summarized our hours and expenses. I'd eliminated Jen's hours for this morning because that might bring up questions I wanted to avoid, and there were no extraordinary expenses. He closed the report and looked out the window for several moments then at me. He took a checkbook out of his coat.

"Looks like I owe you another $450."

"We're a business. The local police won't charge you for their help."

"True, but aside from locating Ryker's truck and the sighting of Tessa at the bus station, you've come closest to locating her so far. And my wanderings haven't produced any results."

"Where have you looked?"

"Some teen hangouts Sergeant Wainwright suggested. That Westbrook Mall you mentioned. El Mercado over on the Westside. Riverside Park. Then a couple soup kitchens, a homeless shelter and a makeshift campground along the river north of the city. So. You don't come cheap, but if you're willing, I'd like you to continue looking for her."

"We can do that."

"Thank you. I really want to find that girl. Find out why she's too scared to come to us. Find the bastard she's running from. I'm booked at the motel until Sunday noon. Then I need to head home. What's it going to cost to hire you till then?"

"How about you pay the four-fifty and another fifteen hundred retainer. I'll update you tomorrow unless something breaks sooner. We can decide what to do then if we don't have any new leads. I imagine your family's anxious to have you home."

"Not really. It's just me and the boys. My wife passed a few years back."

"Sorry for your loss."

"Thank you. I've pretty much gotten used to it. Actually, there's just Jeff at home now and he's having a good time staying at a friend's this week. John, my oldest, joined the Air Force recently and is down in Texas for basic training."

He wrote out a check and handed it to me.

"I want you to know how much I appreciate all the time and effort you all have given this. If anyone finds Tessa Ryker, I think it'll be you."

"We do our best."

"I'm sure you do." He tapped the report. "You know, I think that woman at the diner may be the key. I think they must have met earlier. She gave Tessa that cap and sent her to the diner. Couldn't go with her for some reason at the time. Maybe a shift worker. Something like that. I bet you find her, you find Tessa. Anyhow, I need to go see Sergeant Wainwright."

He took the report, shook our hands, picked up the trash bag with Tessa's things and left.

Jen came over to us. "Wow. He doesn't act like a killer."

"I'm not sure how a killer acts."

Barb picked up the check from where I'd left it on the coffee table.

"One thing's for sure. He's spending a lot of his own money. How much do sheriffs make?"

Jen headed for the door. "Give me a minute and I'll let you know."

"What do you think, Rachel? Good guy or bad guy?"

"I'm not sure. Jen made some very valid points earlier, but he seems awfully sincere about wanting the girl safe. If that sincerity is phony, he's the best damn actor I've met."

"That's my problem too. I like him. And yet . . ."

"Right. 'And yet.' That's the question. They say Ted Bundy was likable too, so who knows."

"Who's Ted Bundy?"

"Serial killer back in the seventies. Killed at least thirty women."

"Oh. Did you notice how he kept calling Detective Anderson by her first name?"

"Yes, why?"

"Think they're having an affair?"

"Maybe, but 'affair' suggests something improper. He's a widower, so a relationship shouldn't matter unless she's married or there's a policy against it with him being her boss."

"If he's the killer, would she cover for him?"

"Love makes people do strange things. We don't know they're in a relationship, but what do you think? You talked with her. What's your impression?"

"She seems straight to me. She's positive Tessa is innocent, and I think she wants to find the real killer. But this was just one conversation on the phone. I don't know."

"Too many questions."

Jen came back. "According to a public notice of the Blank County Employee's Salaries and Job Titles for 2018, Sheriff Donahue's salary is just over twenty-five hundred dollars biweekly."

"You're amazing."

"Aren't I though?"

Barb looked at the check. "And he's paid us more than thirty-four hundred. That's —"

"Nearly three weeks salary," Jen finished. "That's a lot of bread, and no matter how you slice it, that's suspicious to me. Can't see why he'd do it, friends or not."

"It's a chunk. Let's do a background on him and see if anything odd pops up. At least with a first name like Baxter, we shouldn't get many. It can wait till later if you two want to get something to eat."

"What about you? We could go to Phil's."

"Can't. Got another client coming in half an hour."

"Right. Another Terry wasn't it?"

"Terry Romer. Let's run a check on him too. Nineteen to twenty-four I think. Could be Terrence with one or two Rs. Romer: R-O-M-E-R."

"Got it."

"Barb, regarding what we just talked about, why don't you check out Anderson then see what you can find on that Anonymity group. We can all go to Phil's after the meeting with Romer. My treat."

"Didn't you tell Ruth we'd be over for spaghetti night?"

"You're right, I did. I'll treat you guys another time."

While Barb and Jen were busy, I called Sgt. Wainwright. I was put on hold. I idly flipped through the Ryker file waiting.

"Sergeant Wainwright."

"Howard, it's Rachel Cord."

"Hey, lady. We keep passing each other. Any luck locating Tessa Ryker?"

"A bit. Found her sports bag and clothes at Salvation Army. Gave them to Sheriff Donahue. Said he was headed your way and he'd drop them off so your lab could go over them."

"He said he was coming by. Hasn't gotten here yet. Is the stuff contaminated?"

"Not by me. I used gloves and a clean trash bag. Can't speak for Salvation Army though. It was dumped in one of their collection bins."

"Probably useless then, but we'll look. Her parka too?"

"Yeah. Shoes too. Looked like everything to me."

"Dang. That makes her harder to find. Anything else?"

"No. Just wanted to stay in touch."

"Okay. Thanks for the update. Catch you later."

Jen came back. "Nothing bad on the sheriff. No major debts or bankruptcies. Family originally from Texas. Father worked in the oil industry. Came north to work in the Nebraska oil fields. Nothing as to why he quit, but the family settled in Hartfield in eighty-one. Both parents deceased. The sheriff must have inherited the house. No mortgage. Never lived anywhere else. And I couldn't find anything on Terry Romer. The only Romer that came up was a former governor of Colorado and he has no Terrys listed as relatives."

"Okay. How's Barb doing?"

"She was grumbling a lot. She's on the phone now."

I glanced at the clock. "Romer should be here any time now. Make fresh coffee, please, and stash the rest of the donuts. He sounded pretty young, how's our soda supply?"

"Coke, Pepsi, Sprite and Vernor's."

While Jen made coffee, I put the Ryker files away and got out a blank contract.

Ryker's duffel was empty. *The girl must have the money. So where is it? How much has she spent? What's she using it for? Paying people like that woman at the diner? Is that how she's been able to hide?*

Who is that woman? What's Tessa Ryker to her? The money. Has to be the money. Why else would she help her? Does she *have it now? Damn it, I need that money.*

Those PIs need to find her. Why didn't they go looking for her right away? They're smart. It's a hot lead. Why wait? Did they want to be sure they'd get paid more? Or did they wait? Do they know who she is? Are they stalling? Lying? Do they know about the money? Was there something in that duffel . . . Are they after it too? My money! I got to find that girl.

Eighteen

Terry sat outside the library using its Wi-Fi and googled the best route to the detective's office. He had 20 minutes to wait for the bus across the street and would have another wait when he transferred at the downtown terminal. No one was around, so he opened his backpack and counted out $1,500 and put it in a side pocket. He got up and crossed to the bus stop.

The bus let Terry off at the corner of Central Boulevard and Cutter Avenue. It was only a few blocks walk to Mann Avenue. He checked the time. He had nearly an hour before his appointment.

Should I go now? Would she see me early?

He looked around to see if anyone were watching him. The loaded gun and the $10,000 he was carrying made him nervous. The only person who had gotten off the bus when he did—a woman—was headed west and didn't look back.

Across the street was the largest oak he'd ever seen. It looked out of place on the busy business streets. Beneath it were a few picnic tables where people were sitting and eating. In its shadow was a small take-out restaurant—little more than a shack—from which emanated the pleasant aromas of grilling hot dogs, frying potatoes and spicy chili. Terry waited for the light to change and walked over.

The sign above the shack said Charlie's Chicago Hot Dogs. There was a small menu posted next to the take-out window: *Chicago Dog, Slaw Dog, Chili Dog, Chili Slaw Dog, Chili Cheese Dog, Bowl of Chili. Sides: French Fries, Chili Cheese Fries, Slaw.* Taped to the window a faded notice in large red letters stated, NO KETCHUP!

Terry ordered the chili cheese fries and a large Mountain Dew and sat at an empty picnic table. He glanced around and set his backpack between his legs. No one was paying any attention, but he was afraid everyone could tell he was hiding something.

He sipped his drink and began eating. The fries were hot and crisp and the chili flavorful. Terry started to relax and enjoy his meal when a police car pulled to the curb.

A police officer got out on the passenger side. Terry ducked his head and kept eating. The officer stopped by his table.

"How's the chili today?"

Terry swallowed and looked up. "Ah . . . really good."

The officer nodded and went up to the window. He was handed a paper bag and he paid. On his way back he held up the bag.

"Best chilidogs in town. Enjoy your meal."

Terry hardly breathed for several minutes after the police car drove away. He took a deep drink and sighed with relief. No one else gave him any notice. After a few more minutes, he finished the fries and drink. He tossed the used containers in the trash and headed for Mann Avenue.

Mann Avenue Plaza was an imposing, three story building with tall windows on each floor. There was a parking lot in front marked for visitors, and Terry had noticed another lot along the side as he approached. After a moment's hesitation, he adjusted his backpack, squared his shoulders, went up the broad steps and entered.

The plaza lobby was huge and open to the second floor as well as the rear of the building where tall windows and glass doors looked out onto a large courtyard. Hallways led left and right and two staircases went to the second floor. Signs pointed to elevators and public restrooms. On one wall was the building's history with pictures. In the center of the lobby was the building directory.

Terry consulted the directory and went up the staircase to his right. At the top of the stairs, two women were working at a large round reception station. One of the women looked up.

"May I help you?"

"Yes. I'm looking for Rachel Cord."

"Do you have an appointment?"

"Yes, I do. Three o'clock."

The woman looked at a sheet on her desk.

"You must be Terry Romer. It's down the hall on your right. Room 222. Confidential Investigations is on the door."

"Thank you."

Terry started down the hallway, stopped and turned back.

"Excuse me. Is there a bathroom I could use?"

"Yes. Right over there."

"Thank you."

Terry almost entered the women's bathroom before catching his mistake. He looked over his shoulder but neither woman was watching him. He went in the men's room. No one was there. He went and leaned on a sink and stared at himself in the mirror.

Stay calm. You can do this. You're Terry Romer. Remember that. Not Tessa Ryker. Terrence Mayhew Romer from Colorado. You're only looking for Sheriff Donahue. That's all. The detective just has to locate him. That's all. Just locate him and tell you where to find him.

Terry washed his face and hands and dried them. He took off his backpack and looked around. No one had come in, but he was still nervous. He went into a stall and locked the door. He took the $1,500 out of his backpack and put it in his pants pocket. He looked at himself one last time before leaving the room.

He knocked on the door to Confidential Investigations and someone inside said to come in. To his right there were two upholstered chairs and a loveseat arranged in a U with a low coffee table in the middle. On the left were several filing cabinets with a wall-mounted television set above it and a door to another room. Beyond the sitting area was a woman sitting at a desk who looked vaguely familiar. Behind her were cloth cubical panels hiding the rest of the office, but Terry could see the high windows over them. The woman put down the phone she was holding and stood. Terry thought she looked surprised. Then he remembered where he had seen her. He started to back out the door.

"Hi. You must be Mr. Romer." She gave him a reassuring smile.

Terry still held the door handle not sure if he should stay or flee.

"Please, come in. We've been expecting you."

"Are . . . are you Rachel Cord?"

Terry cursed himself silently. This was obviously not the woman whose picture he'd seen on television.

"No. I'm Barbara Lange, Ms. Cord's associate."

At the doorway to his left another woman appeared. It was the other one he'd seen earlier. He saw her eyes widen slightly then she came forward with a large smile and her hand out.

"You're a pleasant surprise." She took his hand firmly, shaking it and virtually pulling him into the room. "I'm Jennifer Hackett. We met briefly this morning at the library."

Terry nodded dumbly.

A third woman appeared. She was his height wearing a man's charcoal gray, pinstriped suit. Her hair was dark blonde cut in a feathered pixie with silver highlights. She was older than the picture he'd seen.

"Mr. Romer, good afternoon. I'm Rachel Cord. It's a pleasure meeting you. Why don't we go in my office and you can tell me how I can help you?"

The woman led him into the other room. He was surprised to see six student tables and chairs set in two rows, a large blackboard and a schoolhouse clock, and a teacher's desk that looked exactly like the one Mrs. Andrews had in her social studies classroom. The woman went to the high windows where two loveseats faced each other and motioned toward one.

"Please sit and take your backpack off so you'll be comfortable. Would you like something to drink? There's fresh coffee or we have water or soda if you prefer."

Terry glanced briefly behind him. The other two women had followed him into the room. He remembered seeing them at the library and outside Walgreens by a red and black sports car. He remembered seeing the car also parked at the library and coming out of the apartment complex. Were these the people Paula warned him about? He felt suddenly trapped.

"Mr. Romer? Are you all right?"

"Ah," Terry's mouth was dry. "Ah, yeah. I'm fine." He swallowed. "Ah, do you have Mountain Dew?"

"Sorry, we don't."

"Dr. Pepper?"

The woman made a sour expression then smiled. "No. We have Pepsi or Coke and Sprite or ginger ale."

"Ah," he wet his lips. Was it getting hot? "Some water, please. Thank you."

"Please sit. Be comfortable. We're here to help you."

Terry slipped off his backpack and sat placing it between his feet. The woman sat opposite and laid a legal pad and a clipboard with a form on it on the coffee table. The tall blond woman — Barbara was it? — sat on the arm of the opposite loveseat and rolled her eyes when the shorter woman — Jennifer — handed him a bottle of water and sat beside him.

The women were looking at him. He wasn't sure how to begin. He began thinking coming here was a bad idea. He uncapped the water and took a long drink.

The woman leaned forward. "Your name is Terry, right? May I call you that?"

He wasn't sure if Paula had fooled the two women or not, but for now, he'd just have to play it out.

"Yes, ma'am. It's really Terrence but everyone calls me Terry."

"Okay, Terry. I'm Rachel. On the phone you indicated you were in a hurry to locate someone."

Maybe this could still work if they don't suspect who I am.

"Yes, ma'am. As soon as possible. Right away would be great."

"I'm sure it would be. How old are you, Terry?"

"Nineteen, but don't let that worry you. I can pay your rates. I have it right here." He started to reach into his pants pocket.

"That's not necessary yet. Do you live here?"

"No, ma'am. Just visiting. I'm from Colorado. Boulder."

Jennifer's eyes widened. "Is—"

Rachel cut her off. "Is the person you're seeking from Colorado also? Are you related in some way?"

"No, ma'am. We're not related. I just need to find him and talk with him."

"And you think he's here and that we can locate him quickly?"

"Yes, ma'am. I know he's here and I'm sure he'll be easy to find. I just don't know how to do it. Don't know where he's staying. I figure it'd be simple for you."

"How do you figure that?"

"You're detectives and he was on TV last night. He's that sheriff from Nebraska looking for that girl."

Jennifer and Barbara looked at each other then at Rachel and then back at Terry.

"Do you mean Sheriff Baxter Donahue from Blank County?"

"Yes, ma'am. That's him. Think you can find him today?"

"Definitely, but why do you need to see him? Do you have information about the whereabouts of Tessa Ryker?"

"Oh, no, ma'am. It's not about her." Terry wet his lips. "It's, it's a personal matter."

"Do you know Sheriff Donahue?"

"Ah . . . no, not exactly, that is—I saw him on TV, but I haven't, haven't . . ."

"Terry, I'm confused. You're from Boulder, Colorado, and he's from Hartfield, Nebraska. What personal matter would you two have if you don't know him??"

Terry felt Rachel was staring at him intently. Jennifer was sitting close to him. Too close. She made him nervous. She and Barbara were looking at him too. This wasn't going the way he expected. He desperately tried to think of an explanation, something to get the conversation away from Tessa Ryker. There was something in that book he'd read about Rachel.

"He . . . he, the sheriff . . . he tried to . . . made a pass at me."

"What?"

The "What" sounded especially loud as all three women said it together. Terry began nodding.

"He did. Yesterday. We met . . . met and he bought me dinner. Then he wanted me to go to his hotel with him and . . . and . . . and he put his hand . . . I can't say it."

Terry lowered his head and covered his eyes with his hand. Shit. What a stupid thing to say. No one was talking. I gotta get out of here. He grabbed his backpack and stood.

"This was a mistake. I'm sorry."

He headed for the door.

"Wait a minute."

He turned. "I shouldn't have said that. I'm sorry. I shouldn't have come here. It's all a big mistake. I . . ."

His voice was cracking and eyes tearing. Rachel came and looked at him closely.

"Sheriff Donahue didn't try to molest you yesterday, did he?"

Tessa shook her head. "Worse. He killed my family. I saw him."

Nineteen

The young man in front of me suddenly turned into a very young and frightened girl.

"Tessa?"

She nodded. Her shoulders sagged and she dropped her backpack. There was a loud clunk when it hit the floor. I took her in my arms. She clung to me, her face buried against my shoulder, her voice muffled.

"Don't . . . don't turn me in, please. Please. He'll kill me too. I know he will."

"No one's going to kill you. I said we're here to help you and we will. Let's go sit down and talk about it."

As I settled Tessa back on the loveseat, Barb caught my attention. She'd picked up the backpack and opened it. She made the shape of a gun with her hand and indicated the backpack. Then she rubbed her thumb and fingers together to indicate money. Jen came over with a cup of coffee and the rest of the donuts and sat next to Tessa.

"Here. Drink this. It's hot chocolate. I made it extra sweet. It'll help. Careful though, it's hot."

Tessa took a sip and then another.

"You made a pretty convincing guy, you know? Had me fooled. Really liked your voice.

While Jen made nice with Tessa, I went to Barb. She spoke quietly.

"There's a pistol in here. I'm guessing the murder weapon, and there's lots of money. Must be thousands. Where'd she get that?"

"We'll have to ask her when she's ready. Let's take a look."

We went to my desk and put on vinyl gloves then emptied the backpack.

The gun was a 9mm Beretta. From the stamping, it must have been military issued at one time. The serial number could be traced to learn its history. The safety was on. I removed the clip and checked the chamber. It was empty. The clip was a new 15-round, Mec-Gar magazine and appeared fully loaded. There was a second Mec-Gar magazine in the bag also fully loaded. A partially-loaded Beretta magazine and a single bullet were in a plastic baggie. I held it up.

"This is interesting."

"Why's it bagged?"

"Evidence?"

"Would she know to do that?"

I shrugged and looked over to Tessa. Jen had her actually laughing. I went back to the backpack. Barb counted the money. $8,500. All hundreds in two stacks wrapped with rubber bands. Where does a 14-year-old get that kind of money? There was a laptop computer with power cord and charger. There were two chargers for cellphones but no phone. Sticking out of a side pocket was a tightly rolled magazine. It was a copy of Cosmo. I laid it aside. There was a 9x12 manila envelope in an inside sleeve. I opened it. Inside were a birth certificate, a rent receipt for an apartment in Boulder, Colorado, a Selective Service card and a voter registration card. All were in the name of Terrence Mayhew Romer. I held the birth certificate up to the light and saw the official embossed seal.

"Curiouser and curiouser."

Barb pointed to Donahue's check still sitting on my desk.

"What are we going to do about that? Should we tell her he hired us to find her?"

"Not yet. We need her to trust us. Let's hear what she has to say first."

We left the things on my desk and went over to the loveseats. The donuts were gone and the empty coffee cup was on the table. Tessa looked up without raising her head.

"Would you like something more to drink?"

"No, thank you."

Barb and I sat. "You say you saw Sheriff Donahue kill your family?"

Tessa sat back. "Not *see* exactly. I saw him come out of the house right after I heard the shots. He got in his SUV and left. *Why* would he do that if he didn't kill them?"

"A very good question."

"And the *gun* was in my dad's *wrong* hand."

She was becoming agitated.

"Okay, let's back up. Calm down. Tell us what you saw and did. Start at the beginning. Why weren't you in school?"

Tessa took several breaths and wetted her lips. She asked for more water and Jen brought it. She took several sips.

She told us about her problems with her boyfriend and that she'd skipped school to try and figure things out. Jen muttered, "Creep," but otherwise we didn't interrupt. She told us of hearing the shots, of seeing the sheriff, finding her family's bodies, sitting with her sister, realizing that she was a witness but couldn't report the crime. The sheriff would know she saw him. So she ran away.

"You were at the edge of the woods when you saw the sheriff. How far away was that?"

"It's a big field. A hundred yards, maybe."

"That's pretty far. How were you sure it was him?"

"His SUV. It has special markings on the side so you know it's him and not just one of his deputies."

"Tell me again about the money your dad hid in the barn."

"It was in an Army bag with his name on it. I counted it. There's over two hundred thousand dollars. I think there was more. I remember the bag being fuller when he hid it."

"Any idea where it came from?"

"Afghanistan? Where else it could have come from. Dad hid it when he came home, and we've never made that much extra money on our crops. I think the sheriff knew about it and wants it. They were over there together."

"The money in your backpack, is it part of what was hidden?"

Tessa nodded. "Yes. Thought I'd need some to hire you, and . . . if things didn't go as planned, I'd have some till I got back for the rest."

"Where's that?"

Tessa didn't answer and I let it go for the moment. I had a fair idea where it was.

"Okay. That gun in your backpack. It's the murder weapon?"

"I think so. It's what the sheriff left in my dad's hand."

"The wrong hand."

"Right. Because of his eyes, Dad always shot right-handed."

"Why did you take it?"

"Because the sheriff made it look like Dad shot Mom and Trina and then himself. It's not true and I didn't want anyone to think it was.""

"What's your plan?" Tessa didn't answer right away. "You wanted me to find the sheriff, right? What then? Were you going to kill him with the same gun that killed your family?"

"Only if he wouldn't confess." She stared at us defiantly. "He *killed* my parents! My sister! He doesn't deserve to live."

"You're probably right, but that's not for you to decide. Trust me. Killing someone isn't easy and will haunt you forever."

"I read that book about you. Was it true?"

"Mostly. Andy stretched things here and there, but mainly he told the truth."

"Do you believe I'm telling the truth?"

I glanced at Barb and Jen. "Yes, we do."

"Will you help me prove he did it?"

"Absolutely!" Jen said. She looked at me. "We are, aren't we?"

"I can pay you." Tessa reached into her pocket again.

"Stop. Please. We're going to help you. Leave your money alone." Kids. "So you took the gun to confuse things."

"Yes. I was afraid they'd believe what they saw and not investigate."

"Well, they're investigating and they don't think your dad killed anyone."

"Honest?"

"Cross my heart. Two magazines in your bag are new. Were they with the gun or in your house?"

Tessa blushed. "No. I bought them here."

"Really? Okay. The ammo too?"

"Uh-huh."

"Unbelievable. Who sells ammunition to fourteen-year-olds?"

"He thought I was older."

"We did too," Jen added.

"All right. What about the magazine in the baggie?"

"That was in the gun when I took it."

"Why did you put it in a baggie?"

"I read an article and watched a video online. It said fingerprints, and maybe DNA too, can be found on the clip or bullets. I thought it could be evidence."

"Smart. Good job. Did you handle the magazine or the bullets?"

"No. The video showed how to release the clip right into the bag. I picked the bullet up with a tissue. It flew out when I pulled back the slide."

"My God," Jen said. "That's scary."

"Fuck yeah. Sorry. It could have gone off the whole time I had it."

"You didn't put the safety on when you took it?"

"I didn't know anything about that kind of gun before watching the videos. Didn't know what a safety was. All I've ever used was my four-ten and only with Dad. It doesn't have a safety. Yeah. That bullet scared me totally."

"I'd have peed my pants."

"For real?"

"Oh, yeah."

We all laughed nervously.

"It's too bad," Barb said. "

"What is?"

"About the gun. We have it and it might have fingerprint evidence. Forensics proves Ryker couldn't have fired all the shots, and Tessa can testify she saw the gun in her dad's left hand."

"And?"

"I just wish there was some other way to corroborate it."

"I took pictures. Of my dad with the gun. On my phone."

"The police have your phone and found no pictures."

"I deleted everything when I ditched the phone. But I saved them to the cloud."

"The police know all your accounts."

"Maybe not this one. It's not linked to my email or any of my accounts. I . . . Brian was bugging me about having sex. I'm not ready for that, but I thought sexting him photos would make him happy so I set up a cloud account in Trina's name to store them. I never took the pictures though. The ones of my dad are all that's there."

"Can you access them?"

"Sure. Give me my computer."

Barb brought the laptop over. Tessa booted it, connected to our Wi-Fi and went to her cloud account. There were two photos there. One showed Terry Ryker's body on the floor holding the Beretta in his left hand. It must have been very difficult for Tessa to take that picture. She didn't look too comfortable seeing it now either. The other photo was a close-up of Ryker's left hand and the gun. These were good supporting evidence but a lot more would be needed to convince a DA to arrest a sheriff.

"I'm sorry I didn't take a picture of the sheriff standing on our porch."

"You were scared. Didn't know what was happening. Don't beat yourself up over it. Can you send these to us? They'll be a big help."

"Sure. What's your address?"

"Let me do it."

Jen turned the laptop and rapidly downloaded the photos to our system then did some things to Tessa's settings and logged out. She wrote something on my pad, tore it off and gave it to Tessa.

"Your sister's birthday isn't a very strong password. I changed it and added a second for two-step verification. I also changed your user name. No one's getting into your account except you."

"Zanzibar57? What's that have to do with me?"

"Absolutely nothing. That's the point."

"Thanks." Tessa looked at all of us. "Thank you so much for believing me. You don't know how crazy it's been pretending to be a guy and trying to find a way to catch the sheriff."

Barb gave me a look and mouthed silently, "Tell her."

This was a dilemma. Tessa did need to be told, but was this the right moment? Would she continue to trust us or try and bolt again? There were a lot of things I wanted to know first. Like where did she get such legitimate looking ID papers? Those things aren't cheap or easy to come by. Was that group Barb mentioned—Anonymity—involved? Did they have those kinds of resources? Will I get answers if I tell her? The looks Barb and Jen were giving me said, "Do it." What the hell? In for a penny, in for a pound.

Twenty

"Tessa. It may seem crazy, but you managed to stay hidden for more than two weeks. That was a hell of an accomplishment for anyone in your situation much less someone your age. But it's good you came to us when you did. To be honest, we were looking for you already, and we were getting close to finding you."

Tessa started to get up.

"Please wait. Hear me out. Believe me when I say we're on your side."

Tessa looked accusingly at Jen and Barb.

"You were at Paula's and the library. You're after the reward like she said." She looked back at me. "Why should I trust anything you say?"

"That you'll have to decide for yourself. We're not after any reward, but if you're not going to trust us, then you'd better go back to Ms. Fowler's right now, get your money and get out of this city as fast as you can."

Her eyes widened. "How . . . how do you know my money's there?"

"Where else would you leave it? You've been hiding out with her pretending to be her cousin, right? You didn't bury it or rent a storage locker somewhere now did you? Well?" She shook her head. "I didn't think so. Does she know about the money?"

"No. I didn't tell her about it?"

"Why not?"

"I . . . I was afraid. It had to be stolen money. Why else would Dad have hidden it? I didn't . . . didn't want her to think my father was bad and deserved to die. She's been very good to me. Protected me. I didn't want to disappoint her."

"Does she know you have the gun?"

"No. I told her about the murders and the sheriff. She knows how badly I want him arrested. If she knew about the gun, she'd try to take it away. She knows I'd try to kill him if I could."

"Does she know you're here?"

"No. After *their* visit, Paula got very worried. She wants to get me out of town right away—today—but I told her I had to be somewhere first. I didn't say where or why just that it was too important. She's waiting for me to take me . . . to a safe place."

"I don't want to know where. I hope it is safe, for your sake, if it's what you decide. Hers too."

"What do you mean, 'hers too'?"

"We found her looking for you. Others will too." Stop stalling. Bite the bullet. "The thing is, the sheriff knows about her. Doesn't know who she is yet, but knows she was seen with you. And the reason he knows is we told him."

"What? How—"

"Please sit down and listen. We want to help you, remember? Half the police forces in the country are looking for you. Until your truck was found a few days ago and video of you at the bus station showed up, no one had a clue where you were, and that information was nearly two weeks old.

"Sheriff Donahue said he wanted to try something different. He hired us yesterday because we have a good reputation for finding lost or runaway teens in this town. Believe me, police hiring private investigators is very unusual. Practically unheard of. That should have been a red flag but it wasn't. He said he was a family friend and wanted you safe. I believed him. My mistake.

"While looking for you, we became uneasy—no, Jen and Barbara became uneasy and suspicious of the sheriff. There were things that didn't seem quite right. Because of that, when we briefed him—just an hour ago here, by the way—we didn't tell him who Paula was or that we'd already spoken with her. We wanted to check him out further. Now, after listening to you, I believe our suspicions are right.

"You saw him. You've given us physical evidence that may link him to the crime. I have to figure some way to get that evidence to the right people to be tested without alerting him. In the meantime, you need to be protected and, I believe, your friend Paula does too. She knows what happened, and that makes her a danger to the killer."

"Oh, God. I didn't think of that. I told her everything. I need to warn her."

Tessa pulled a flip phone out of her vest pocket.

"Wait a minute. Paula's expecting you at the apartment, right?"

"Yes. I said I'd be back in time for her to take me to . . . the safe place before she goes to work tonight."

"I suggest we take you there now. It'll be less complicated speaking to her in person. You two need to make decisions and we need to know if you'll trust us to help. Okay?"

Tessa bit her thumb as she stared at her phone. She had to believe the decision was hers. I needed her trust and it would be easier to gain Paula's that way.

Tessa nodded. "Okay."

"Good. Thank you. Jen get me two large evidence bags and large labels. Barb. Open the safe. We'll secure the evidence there for now."

Barb looked at me and silently mouthed, "guns?" I nodded. Our personal weapons were kept in the safe. We rarely need to carry, but we both recognized this could be one of those times. I didn't know if Sheriff Donahue would wait for us to find Fowler or if he had other means of locating her. I was hoping we had another day but wanted to be ready for anything.

Barb went to the closet with the safe. Jen brought me the bags, labels and a fine-point marker.

"Thanks, Jen. Would you print out copies of the two photos Tessa took?

"Tessa. Write on this label where and when you found this gun and that it's been solely in your possession from then until now. Write small and sign it with today's date. That's good. On this other label write that this clip and bullets were the ones that were in the gun when you found it and have been in your sole possession till now. Also date and sign it."

While she did that, I felt Barb lift the back of my jacket and tuck my S&W 340PD and holster at the small of my back. She also slipped a speedloader with five additional rounds into my jacket pocket. I signed and dated the labels stating I took possession of the items directly from Tessa Ryker. I put gloves back on and put the empty Beretta in one bag and the bag with the Beretta magazine and bullet in the other. I sealed both bags with the labels and gave them to Barb along with the two Mec-Gar magazines to put in the safe.

Jen brought the photograph copies and I had Tessa write on the backs what they were and when she took them. She and I both signed and dated them.

"Tessa, you can put everything else back in your bag. Jen, have Barb put these in the safe too."

"What about this?" Tessa was holding the $8,500.

"Until proven otherwise, it was your dad's and now it's yours. Put it in the bag. And put your game face on. We're going out in public. You need to be Terry Romer a little longer."

Tessa straightened and her face subtly changed, and I was looking at the young man I'd originally met again. Amazing.

"Yes, ma'am."

"Ooh, I love that voice," Jen said.

I shook my head. Kids. "All right, we're ready to go. We'll take the Beamer. It's larger."

As we left, I took two forms from a filing cabinet in the other office.

The drive to Paula Fowler's apartment was uneventful. Tessa as Terry called out as she opened the door and we entered.

"Paula? I'm back."

A magenta-haired, young woman came out of the bedroom.

"I'm glad you're — what are *they* doing here?"

"Ms. Fowler, I'm Rachel Cord. Barbara Lange and Jennifer Hackett work for me. Your *cousin* here wanted to hire me to find Sheriff Baxter Donahue. Would you know anything about that?"

Tessa blushed deeply and turned back into herself as Paula glared at her.

"No. I don't. But I'm quite sure you know she's not my cousin."

"No, she's not, but she has some damn good ID saying she's a guy from Colorado. Know anything about that?"

"Not a clue. What do you want?"

"All kidding aside, Tessa told us about her family's murders and seeing the sheriff at the house. We believe her and want to help her prove he's the killer. The problem is Sheriff Donahue hired us to find Tessa. That's why Barbara and Jennifer spoke with you this morning.

"I briefed the sheriff this afternoon before Tessa came to me, and — for reasons I won't go into right now — we didn't tell him about interviewing you. All he knows at the moment is that she and an unknown woman had breakfast at Belle's Diner two weeks ago. Of course, he wants us to find you, but that's not going to happen now."

"It isn't?"

"No. But the sheriff could have other ways to find you now that he knows about you. Tessa's in danger from him and I think you are too."

"Why am I in danger?"

"Because Tessa told you what happened."

"And the three of you are here to protect me, is that it?"

"If necessary. Tessa says you have a safe place for her to hide. Can you go there too?"

"Did she tell you where?"

"No, she didn't and I didn't ask."

"I wanted her to get out of the state, but she's insisted on staying because of the sheriff. I thought my friend's place would be safe for a few days. Now I'm not sure. I don't want to put my friend in jeopardy too. And I'm not going anywhere. This is my life. Besides, I need to work tonight."

"I don't think that's a good idea, but, as you say, it's your life. As for Tessa, let's not endanger your friend. I know a safe place until this is resolved."

"That might be best. That's all her stuff in that bag."

Paula went and put her arms around Tessa. Tessa buried her face on her shoulder and hugged her back.

"You're a crazy kid, you know that?"

"I'm sorry. I didn't know you'd be in danger too."

"I'll be fine."

"Can't you come too?"

Paula shook her head. "This is my life. I'm not running again. Go. I'll be fine, really. We'll get together when this is over. Promise." She turned to me. "Keep her safe or I'll come after you."

"I'm sure you will. There's a couple more things we need to do though."

"What's that?"

"Whatever happens, you're both going to need legal advice and I know a good lawyer." I took out the forms I'd brought.

"I can't afford a lawyer."

"Not a problem. Tessa's paying for it."

"How? She doesn't have that kind of money."

I pointed to the bag on the futon. "There's over two hundred thousand in that bag. Right, Tessa?" She nodded. "That's one of the reasons the sheriff is after her. He wants the money. It's why he's going to be looking for you too."

"I'm not running."

"Hiding isn't running. It's playing it safe."

"Thanks, but no thanks. Who's your lawyer?"

"Carmen Andrews. She and her partner have represented me for years and I often do investigative work for them. Sometimes, like now, that means signing up a client for them before they've even met them. The two of you just need to sign these forms. Tessa. You can give me that money now that's been burning a hole in your pocket. It'll be Carmen's retainer."

"It's that easy?"

"It's that easy. Let me make a call while you sign the papers."

I stepped outside and called Carmen.

"Hi. I just signed up two new clients for you."

"Hello to you too. What makes you think we need more clients?"

"Okay. Maybe it's they need you."

"What's their problem?"

"You know that murdered family in Nebraska and the missing daughter? I found her and the woman who's been hiding her. I believe she didn't kill her family and she gave me possible evidence to prove it. They need legal representation and I need to cover my butt by being your investigator in this instance."

"Ah, the CYA factor. Always applicable when you send me clients. Have they signed contracts?"

"Doing it now and given me a retainer for you. I'll email you photocopies and get the originals and the retainer to you later."

"When can I meet them?"

"If you're available, I can bring the girl over any time. I'm not sure about the woman. I'll ask.

"I'm nearly done for the day, but I can stay awhile. Be here at six."

"Okay. One more question. Would evidence tested by an independent lab hold up in court?"

"What kind of evidence are we talking about?"

"Fingerprint and possibly DNA."

"I can see problems. Why not turn it in to the police and have them test it? Better chain of custody and they have the databases to match against."

"You'll understand why that's not a good idea when you've talked to Tessa."

"I can hardly wait. See you at six."

The contracts were signed and $1,500 was on the table when I came back in. I wrote a receipt for the money then took pictures of the paperwork and emailed it to Carmen.

"Carmen can see us at six. Paula, that gives you plenty of time before you go to work. We can drop you off after or bring you back for your car?"

"I usually walk to and from work. If we finish with the lawyer early enough, you can drop me at Mama Rosa's. Would anyone like something to drink? There's soda or I can make coffee."

"What kind of soda?"

"Dr. Pepper and Mountain Dew."

Twenty-One

The lights at the law offices of Andrews Pfeiffer McLarty & Associates were all lit. The receptionist was gone but several associates were hard at work in the conference room. One saw us and stuck her head out.

"Carmen said to go straight back. She's waiting for you."

"Thanks."

I was surprised Truman Pfeiffer was with her when we went into her office. Thought he was in Washington lobbying with our local LGBTQ. I introduced them to Tessa and Paula and gave Carmen the original signed contracts and retainer. I gave an ultra short summary of my agency's involvement— I'd brief Carmen in detail later—and left the four of them to talk while Barb, Jen and I went back to the lobby.

"Barb, I'm worried about Paula. I don't think she's taking her situation seriously enough. I may be jumping the gun, but I'd like you to birddog her tonight."

"You think the sheriff could find out who she is this fast?"

"Depends how anxious he is. If he waits for us to find her as we said we would, that's one thing. But if he goes looking for her and goes to Belle's, he might talk to one of the waitresses you did. Then he'll know both who she is and that we lied to him."

"Not good."

"No. Not good at all."

"Paula works eleven to seven. If I'm going to watch out for her all night, I better go get some rest. Where you gonna stash Tessa?"

"My place. We have a guestroom she can use. It's a limited access building. Jen, there's no reason for you to stick around. You and Barb can share a taxi back to the office to get your cars."

"Tessa and I get along. I think she trusts me. How 'bout I drive Barb to the office then come back and stay at your place too? I can pick up my car tomorrow."

"All right." I gave her my keys. "They should be in there at least an hour but get back as soon as you can."

They left and I called Wendy to let her know we were having overnight guests and briefly who they were and why.

"Don't wait supper, I'm not sure how late we'll be."

"Call when you're on your way and I'll have something delivered. That way you won't need to stop somewhere."

"Okay, thanks. See you later."

I went to the break room for coffee, but the pot was nearly empty and what was left looked like syrup. I turned it off and checked the fridge instead. I took a diet cola. There were several pizza boxes on a counter, but I wasn't really interested. I went back to the lobby to wait.

There was still my problem of testing the gun and magazine. I'd prefer a private lab, but Carmen was probably right about that causing complications. If I gave them to Wainwright though, he'd tell the sheriff, and Donahue would know I'd found the girl. He'd want to know why I hadn't told him. If he's the killer—as it looks like—he'll fear we're on to him and have to be worried about his fingerprints being discovered. What's he liable to do then?

Would Denise do it for me on the sly? Maybe enter the gun as a "found" weapon and check to see if it's connected to some crime? But how do I explain I don't want Wainwright or Donahue to know without telling her where I got it and Tessa's accusations? Would she trust me enough to go that far out on a limb? Or would she close ranks defending a fellow law officer? And if prints or DNA are found, how do we check them against Donahue's? Are law officers' fingerprints in the national database?

He's been in my office. His prints should be there. And should definitely be on the file he gave us if Barb or I haven't obscured them. I'll need to check in the morning.

I hadn't reached a decision when Jen returned.

"They still in there?"

"Yeah. Were there any messages at the office?"

"I didn't go up. Sorry. Just dropped Barb at her car."

"That's okay. Not your job. I'd have gotten a call if anything were important. If you're thirsty, there's water and soda in the break room."

Jen came back with a bottle of water and slices of pizza on a paper plate.

"Not much choice. Want one? We skipped lunch, remember?"

The pizza slices looked cold and sad. A few dried out veggies and red sauce. No cheese. No pepperoni.

"No thanks. I'll wait till we get home. Wendy's going to have something delivered for us."

"Hope she doesn't order anything fancy or exotic," Jen mumbled through a bite of pizza. She swallowed. "Don't get me wrong. I love everything you guys make or ordered when you had me over. Tessa just strikes me as the burger and fries type, is all."

"Says She-Who-Eats-Anything."

"I'm an omnivore. What do you expect?"

Jen had finished the pizza and was eyeing the candy dish on the receptionist's desk when Carmen came down the hall.

"Tessa tells an interesting story. Do you believe her?"

"Yes. Don't you?"

"Mostly. I believe she believes what she's saying. I'm a little leery on some of the details. You have the gun?"

"In my safe."

"And the money?"

"In her duffel bag in the Beamer. There's also several thousand in her backpack."

"Bring the bag in. We're going to secure the money here."

Jen went to fetch Tessa's bag and I followed Carmen back to her office. Before we entered, she turned.

"What do you think of the sheriff? Apparently you've met him."

"That's how I got involved in the first place. He hired us to find her, which is pretty unusual. We were getting close when she showed up disguised as a guy wanting us to find him. She's convinced he killed her family and wants revenge. The thing is he seems straight but could be fooling me. I don't know for sure. Till I find out more, I'm siding with her."

"Probably best. She was too far away to identify the killer and basing it on a decal on the side of a vehicle is dubious. A defense attorney would make mincemeat of that on cross. It only holds up if there's corroborating evidence like his prints or DNA on the gun, magazine or bullets. What have you decided about turning them in to be tested?"

"I haven't yet. I don't know how to do it without him being warned."

"That is a problem. Any way to check his alibi for the time of the murders without him getting suspicious?"

"There's an idea. I'll think on it. If I can, I'll hang onto the gun awhile longer until we check him out."

"Well work fast. We can't keep Tessa under wraps too long. Where are you taking her?"

"My place. How much time do you think we have?"

"Tomorrow should be good, but by Saturday we're going to have to think seriously about negotiating her turning herself and the gun in. I don't intend to discuss it with her until then. She may try to bolt. After that, it won't matter if the sheriff knows. He'll either be innocent or running if prints are found on the gun."

Jen joined us and we entered the office. There was an open metal briefcase with combination locks on the table and Tessa's money from her backpack was already in it. Carmen had her add what was in her duffel. Tessa set several things aside including the remaining 9mm ammunition and a small blue metal box so she could get to the hidden cash. There were several dozen stacks of twenties and hundreds and a single stack of tens all tied with string or rubber bands. The money more than filled half the briefcase.

Carmen showed Tessa how to change the combinations on the locks and let her pick her own. Then she wrote out a receipt for the money and had Tessa sign it. Truman took the briefcase and left the room.

Carmen asked what was in the metal box. Tessa said family papers like birth certificates and her dad's Army stuff and maybe some cash. She wasn't exactly sure. She hadn't opened it. Asked if she wanted to open it, she shook her head, no. Carmen asked if she wanted her to keep it for her and Tessa nodded. Then Carmen gave Tessa and Paula her standard legal pep talk and we were ready to leave.

On the way to the car, I asked Paula again if she wanted to stay with me too.

"No, thanks. I'm through hiding."

I wasn't sure what she meant and doubted she'd enlighten me.

"Well, if you need to tell anyone again about your breakfast with Tessa pick a more common name than Cindy Lou and don't make her Cajun."

"Is that what screwed me up?"

"Partly."

"How about Carol?"

"Part of her mother's name. That's believable. Fake names are often something familiar or use the same initial. Like using Terry as her guy name was another red flag."

"I thought it might be, but it was her choice. I was trying to win her trust at the time."

"I can understand that. Where'd all the fake ID come from?"

"No idea what you're talking about."

"That's what I thought. Still want to go to Mama Rosa's?

"Please. I'll have dinner and hang out till work."

I called Wendy to let her know when we'd arrive, dropped Paula off and headed home. We Deliver was just leaving as I pulled into the parking lot. Hoped it was for us as I was starving.

The smell of hot fries and onion rings made my mouth water as we entered my condo. Wendy had laid out plates and silverware and was opening two large bags from Bailey's. There were classic cheeseburgers with everything and a chickpea burger for her and chocolate shakes for everyone.

She welcomed Tessa and Jen with huge hugs and seated them then hugged me. She stiffened slightly when she felt my gun still tucked in the small of my back.

"Is that really necessary?" she whispered in my ear.

Aside from a short period when guns and body armor became a daily necessity for both of us, guns have not been a part of our home life. Wendy doesn't like them on principle. They have a single purpose and function: to kill. And while she used one 12 years ago to save us from a man bent on killing me, she prefers not to have them around.

"I hope not, but I can't take chances with protecting Tessa. Sorry."

Dinner went well and Jen kept Tessa distracted all evening. I went online to see if the Blank County Sheriff's site had any type of schedule of events or planning calendar. Anything that'd give me a clue as to where Donahue was the day of the murders. Nada. I was sure it was there just not available to the public.

At 10:45, Barbara called to say she was outside Walgreens and settled in. Paula had arrived and there was no sign of Sheriff Donahue. I told her to call if anything happened or in the morning before Paula's shift ended.

Barbara stretched as best she could in her small car and looked at her watch. Three a.m. A string of customers had been in and out until one, but no one since. She got out of her car and stretched again. The air held a definite chill. Although she was well layered, she was beginning to feel the cold. She jumped up and down several times to get warm and—more importantly—stay awake. Surveillance could be so boring. She walked over to where she could see the checkout register inside the store through the glass doors. No one was there. She moved back and forth straining to see as much of the store as she could but didn't see Paula anywhere.

She hurried in. She looked behind the counter, began looking down aisles.

"Can I help you?"

Barbara turned quickly. Paula had come out of an aisle behind her.

"Ah. Yes. Hi. Um, I need—" What do I need? "Where are your feminine products?"

"Aisle six. In back." Paula suddenly recognized her. "Are you watching me?"

"Watching you? Why would I—"

"You are, aren't you?"

"No. I came in to—"

"Do you people really think that sheriff's gonna come in here and hurt me? Really?"

"No. Of course not. Where would you get—Oh, all right, yes. Yes, we think you're in danger. And you should too. You know perfectly well Tessa's in danger because of what she saw, and now most likely because of the money she has. She's been staying with you for two weeks. It's logical to think she's told you everything, and that makes you a threat to the sheriff. And, he might think *you* have the money."

"But I don't have it. The lawyers do."

"He doesn't know that."

"So you're here to—what—protect me?"

Barbara shrugged. "If necessary."

"Ridiculous. Go home. I don't want you here."

"And yet, here I stay."

"I could call the cops and have you arrested for loitering on private property."

"Yes, you could. And I'd have to give them some story for why I'm watching you, and they'll tell me to move my car and watch from somewhere else. You'll just waste their time and make it harder for me to do my job. Why bother?"

A bell dinged as a customer came in. Paula turned. Barbara eased a hand inside her coat. A man in his thirties wearing a heavy jacket over jeans and boots picked up a shopping basket and came toward her.

"May I help you, sir?"

His hair was mussed and he looked like he'd just got out of bed.

"You have ice cream?"

"Last aisle on the wall."

"How about dill pickles?"

"Center section in the back by the mustard and ketchup."

"Ginger snaps?"

"Not sure. Try with the rest of the cookies center front."

"Thanks."

Paula went behind the counter and Barbara checked out the candy bar display. The man came back a few minutes later with cartons of Rocky Road, Mint Chocolate Chip and Double Fudge Brownie ice cream along with a large jar of dill pickles and a box of ginger snaps. He sighed as he set everything on the counter.

"You saved me a trip to Walmart. Wife's pregnant and gets the damnedest cravings."

Paula rang everything up and the man left. Barbara laid a candy bar and money on the counter.

"I'll be out in my car if you need me."

"Can't get rid of you?"

"Nope."

"Is it cold out there?"

"Not bad. Dropped into the forties, I think."

"You may as well stay in here awhile then."

Customers started trickling in after five and Barbara went back to her car. At 6:45, she called Rachel.

"Everything's quiet. We're going to breakfast when she gets off then I'll drive her home."

"Any chance she'll come here?"

"She says not. If it's all right, I'll try to talk her into letting me crash at her place. That way I can keep an eye on her and you won't need to relieve me."

"Good idea. There are things I need to do this morning. If it doesn't work out let me know. Stay in touch."

When Paula came out, they drove to Belle's. The diner was busy but people were leaving and a booth had just been cleared when they arrived. Donna was working and hurried over when she saw them enter.

"The law's here lookin' for you," she said to Paula.

Twenty-Two

"**Who?**" Barbara asked.

"Guy at the counter talkin' to Jerry. He's real pushy and downright rude. I don't like him. Says he's a sheriff or somethin'."

All Barbara could see was the man's back. He was heavyset, wearing a dark blue anorak and completely bald. Whoever he was, he wasn't Sheriff Baxter Donahue.

"Thanks, Donna. Please don't say you saw us."

"Don't worry. I won't. I don't put up with rude."

On the way to her car, Barbara noticed a GMC pickup with Nebraska plates and a *Support Your Local Sheriff* bumper sticker. When they got in the car, Barbara took a scarf from the glove box and gave it to Paula.

"Here. It'll hide your hair."

Barbara drove across the street and parked at the library to keep the truck in view.

"Is that the sheriff who's after Tessa?"

"Don't know who he is, but he's not the one I met. I need to check something."

Barbara took out her iPad. The library's Wi-Fi wasn't available nor was any other public site. She made a call and put it on speaker.

"Rachel? We've got a problem."

"What happened?"

"We just came from Belle's. Someone claiming to be a sheriff is in there looking for Paula."

"Did he see you?"

"Luckily, no. One of the waitresses stopped us at the door. The guy's back was to us but he's talking to one of my witnesses. We left right away."

"Is it Donahue?"

"That's the thing. No. Wrong shape and the guy's bald with a real attitude problem according to the waitress. However, there's a truck out front with Nebraska plates. What other sheriff would be investigating a Blank County crime?"

"Are you sure he's a sheriff?"

"Yes. He told—no. I'm not sure. Donna said, 'he's a sheriff or something.' She wasn't sure which but didn't like his rudeness. That's why she warned us off."

"You briefed Donahue's detectives. It could be—damn. Don't know why I can't remember the guy's name."

"Joe Kern, but I only spoke with Detective Anderson."

"He's her partner. She probably briefed him and he's following up on our lead."

"Would the sheriff let him? I mean if Donahue's our killer, would he want one of his detectives here looking for Tessa?"

"Maybe Donahue doesn't know. Could be Kern's here on his own initiative. Where are you?"

"Parked across the street. He's still in the diner. I want to see which way he goes when he comes out."

"Don't follow him. Convince Paula to come here."

"Ms. Cord? I'm convinced. I'm willing to avoid contact till the lawyers say otherwise."

"Thanks, Paula. I think that's best."

"Rachel, we'll grab some stuff from Paula's first."

"Okay. See you when you get here."

Barbara put her iPad away and reached behind Paula's seat and grabbed a camera with a zoom lens.

"Aren't we going now?"

"I still want to know who this guy is. We'll wait 'til he leaves."

Barbara zoomed in on the truck's license plate and took pictures.

"Tessa never told me about the money. Where did it come from?"

"She thinks Afghanistan. She remembered watching her dad hide a duffel bag in the barn after he came home and him catching up the bills and paying down their debts. At the time, she thought it was because the farm was producing again. After the murders, she checked and found the money. Apparently her dad was careful spending it considering how much is there."

"How'd the sheriff know about it?"

"They were together in Afghanistan. I figure they either stole it or found it and when Ryker was wounded, they managed to smuggle it back with his stuff."

"So the sheriff wanted his share and killed Ryker because he wouldn't give it to him?"

"I don't think that's quite right. They were in Afghanistan several years ago. I can't see them waiting that long to split the money. Maybe the sheriff blew his share and needs more now for some reason. I don't know. Ah. There's the guy now."

The man came out of the diner. Through the zoom lens Barbara thought he looked angry. She took pictures as he walked to his truck. He stopped, pulled out a cellphone, looked at it and started talking. Suddenly, he looked like he was coughing as he continued talking. He looked around to see if anyone were watching. Barbara took more pictures wishing she could read lips. The man ended the call and slammed a fist against the truck. He got in, peeled out and turned north at the intersection.

Barbara gave Paula the camera and followed.

"Aren't we going to my place?"

"Yes, but I want to see if he's going to Walgreens to trace you first."

The man didn't stop at Walgreens. He continued north until 21st Street dead-ended at North Ferry Avenue. He turned left and pulled into a Holiday Inn Express across from Westbrook Mall. Barbara turned into the mall and parked. She couldn't see where he parked at the hotel and debated going across and checking on him.

"What do we do now?"

Barbara looked at Paula as she put her car in gear.

"We get your things and go to Rachel's."

After talking to Barb, I went back online to the sheriff department site looking for pictures of personnel. All I found were pictures of Donahue, Chief Deputy Wagner and division captains. Wagner was bald, but I couldn't see how he was who Barb saw as he was in charge of the department while Donahue was here.

I did a general search for Detective Joe Kern and found an article and photo in the Blank County Tribune Examiner. The photo showed Kern and a Sgt. Cody Watson outside the Two Rivers Bank in Arlington following a robbery. It was hard to tell from the distance but both men looked bald to me. Another photo in a different issue of the paper showed Watson with deputies William Harvey and Debra Anderson with pink patches on their uniforms for Breast Cancer Awareness Month two years ago. Watson was definitely bald and the right physical type, but why would he be assigned to investigate here? This was Anderson and Kern's case. I didn't find another photo of Kern. I took screen shots of the photos I found to show Barb. For now, I was sticking with the idea it had to be Kern at Belle's.

I looked again at the photo with Anderson. Standing between her fellow deputies, she looked petite and young with her golden blonde hair pulled back and gracious smile. I pictured her with Donahue; thought they'd make a charming couple, but was he taking advantage of her? Would she falsify evidence to protect him?

More questions with no answers.

I woke Jen and Tessa and started breakfast. Breakfast is usually coffee and cereal or a bagel for Wendy and me during the week. With guests I decided on a weekend favorite, pecan waffles and soysage. Wendy came out in blouse and dark slacks as I was putting the waffle mix in the blender.

"Waffles?"

"Yes. Have you time to make your tofu scramble?"

"The board meeting's not until ten. Do we have everything?"

"Yes. I'll prep."

She grabbed an apron. "Let's do it."

I smiled thinking how her staid directors would react seeing their bank president in a red apron with Che Guevara on it.

"Oh, Barb and Paula will be here soon too."

"Okay."

I pulsed the batter a few times and added club soda like my mother does to make for light and crispy waffles then got out onions, garlic, celery and roasted poblano peppers and diced them. Wendy pulled out the large iron skillet and set it on the stove to warm. She turned on the warming oven. She grabbed a large bowl and dumped in three tubs of soft tofu, a cup-and-a-half of chunky salsa, a bunch of spices and mixed it together with a potato masher. I knew turmeric and cumin were in the blend but have never been able to match her southwest scramble for flavor. "It's the bomb," as I would have said in my youth.

Jen came out of the guestroom. "Can I help?"

"Sure. Where's Tessa?"

"Taking a shower."

I gave Wendy what I'd diced and took Jen over to our home office alcove.

"I'm trying to find out if Sheriff Donahue had any alibi for the day of the killings. I'm sure his schedule is in their system but it's not on the public site."

"You want me to hack their system? I thought—"

"Yes, I know. If I contradict myself, I contradict myself. Just do it, okay?"

"I'd feel easier using the computers at the office. Better firewalls. Can it wait?"

"I'd rather know sooner. See what you can do. And don't say anything to Tessa."

"Okay. Let me get my bag."

The aroma of sautéing garlic, onions and peppers filled the room as I set the table and put out the maple syrup, extra salsa, hot sauce and vegan butter. I glanced at the kitchen clock as I went to set up the waffle iron. Barb was running late. Where was she? Had anything happened or was traffic just that slow?

I plugged in the waffle iron then got out another skillet and the soysage. Wendy folded the cooked peppers and onions into her scramble mix, rebuttered the skillet and poured the mixture in. I looked at the clock again. It was probably too early to be worried but I didn't like it. I started the first waffle and turned the soysage to brown. Wendy gently stirred the scramble. Jen was busy at the computer.

"Wow. Something smells really good."

Tessa came in wearing a gray and white checked, button-down shirt and jeans. She still looked like a guy but I could see she'd foregone taping down her breasts.

"There's orange and grapefruit juice in the fridge if you want. Help yourself. The coffee's ready too. All we have is soymilk though. Breakfast will be ready soon."

The first waffle was done. I put it on a tray in the warming oven, started the second and went to see how Jen was doing. She had a USB drive plugged in to the computer.

"Anything?"

"Not yet. Getting in isn't a problem. They're using a standard security software program. Not leaving a trace requires more finesse. Should have something shortly. Is that Wendy's southwest scramble I smell? Yum."

I checked the time again. Where was my phone? The intercom buzzed by the door and on my computer. About time! I didn't want Jen to stop what she was doing so I went to the video display by the door.

The building entry security camera showed Barb and Paula waiting for access. I buzzed the door open giving them access to the inner alcove. The display switched cameras as Barb pressed our condo button at the inner doors. Some residents felt this double security system annoying, but it prevented unwanted people entering the building who had slipped in the outer doors as someone was leaving. This added security was fine with me. I buzzed them in and went to check the waffle.

"Barb and Paula are finally here."

I slid the waffle onto the tray in the warming oven and started a third. Wendy turned the burner off under the scramble skillet.

"Right on time then. This is done."

She pressed the button on the overhead microwave to warm the plates. I went back over to Jen.

"How's it coming?"

"I found my way in. Should only be a couple more minutes."

"Good. Breakfast is ready."

The doorbell rang. Tessa got up from the table.

"I'll get it."

"No. Wait. I'll do it."

I checked the video display of the hallway before opening the door to be sure it was Barb and Paula. Having a gun go off in my face and being nearly killed at my door years ago, I don't take chances. I let them in.

"Welcome. I'm glad you changed your mind."

"Barbara convinced me."

Barb held up an SD card. "Before you ask why we're late, I waited to take pictures of the guy at Belle's and then followed him. He didn't stop at Walgreens so no one ratted out Paula." She took a deep breath. "Mmmm. Did Wendy make breakfast? We're starved."

"Okay, we'll talk later. Make yourself useful and pour the coffee."

Wendy and I loaded the warm plates with half waffles, tofu scramble and soysage. There was more batter left so I started another waffle. Jen gave a "thumbs up" as she went to the table. Hopefully that meant she found what I wanted and not her thoughts on breakfast.

Breakfast was a pleasant diversion. There was no talk of Tessa's situation or her family's murders. After, Paula and Tessa volunteered to clear and clean the dishes, Wendy left for the bank and Jen, Barb and I went to the computer.

I opened the screen shots I'd taken.

"I'm pretty sure the guy at Belle's is Detective Kern, but it's remotely possible it could be Deputy Watson."

Barb leaned over to get a better view and shook her head.

"No, it's neither of them. Here. Load this."

I inserted the SD card and opened the photo file. Barb took the mouse and double-clicked on an image of a man standing beside a black pickup truck.

"That can't be right. Why's he here?"

Twenty-Three

Barb and Jen both said, "Who is it?"

Rather than answering, I went online to the Blank County Sheriff's Department website and clicked on Administration and there was his picture below the sheriff's. Chief Deputy Harold Wagner.

"That's him." Barb pointed to the picture.

"I can see that. But why's he here? He's supposed to be running the department for Donahue."

"Maybe he's suspicious of the sheriff too. Maybe he knows about Donahue and Anderson and thinks she's covering up for him so he's doing his own investigation."

"Maybe not."

We looked at Jen.

"What I mean is—Let me show you. May I sit?"

I got up from the desk and Jen sat at the computer. Barb went and brought chairs from the dining table. Jen opened a file folder on my desktop as we sat on each side of her. She double-clicked on a file.

"This is Sheriff Donahue's schedule for October. As you can see, he was supposed to be at the Nebraska Sheriffs Association Law Enforcement Conference in Kearney from the afternoon of the sixth through noon on the ninth."

"Was he actually there?"

"I was working on verifying that when we broke for breakfast. I found that he did register and was booked at the La Quinta Inn."

"How far from Hartfield is Kearney?"

"About three hours by car."

"So even if he did attend, he could have cut out on the eighth, killed the Rykers and returned to the conference."

"That's true, but only if he was driving his official SUV. Remember? Tessa saw it. If he used his personal car, why would he switch when he got back to Hartfield? His official vehicle would be parked at the sheriff's department, wouldn't it? Would he chance someone seeing him and asking why he was back so soon? The conference is his alibi. And if he did stay at the conference, who's most likely to have been driving his official vehicle?"

"You're thinking his chief deputy. All right. We need to find something that shows whether Donahue was in Kearney near the time of the murders or not and where Wagner was also that day. We should do a background on him as well."

"I can do all that using the computers at the office."

"Don't you need to be at MGT?"

"I worked on my projects last night on my laptop after Tessa went to sleep. I'd already planned to help you today so that's not a problem. I can do this too."

"Okay. Go to it. Thanks."

Jen transferred Donahue's schedule and Barb's photos to her USB drive and ejected it. She got up to leave.

"Wait a sec," Barb said. "How would Wagner know about the money? Isn't that why the Rykers were killed?"

"Maybe the money's a McGuffin."

"A what?"

"A red herring. Tessa found the money and believes that's why her family was killed. We've assumed the same thing. There may be another reason. We don't know."

Jen gathered her things. "You guys work it out. I'm off."

She left. Paula came over.

"Love the apartment. Tessa showed me your private gym. Can I use it?"

"Sure. You need workout clothes? I think Wendy's will fit."

"I brought sweats, thanks. Think I'll work out a bit before hitting the sack. Haven't been to a gym in ages. And thanks for helping Tessa. I was afraid she'd do something stupid."

"Hopefully, we've prevented that."

Paula yawned. "Sorry. Catch you later."

She headed for the bedrooms.

"That should keep them busy for awhile. You said Wagner didn't stop at Walgreens. Where'd he go?"

"The Holiday Inn Express on North Ferry. You know, he looked upset when he left Belle's then he acted kinda weird."

Barb opened all the photos showing Wagner going from the diner to his truck.

"He got a phone call. When he answered he looked like he started coughing while he was talking. And he kept looking around to see if he were being watched. He wasn't coughing earlier as far as I could tell and he stopped as soon as he hung up. I thought it strange."

While a video would have been better, the steady stream of pictures had a flipbook motion effect as I clicked through them. The pictures ended with Wagner hitting the truck. I went through them a second time more slowly. I sat back.

"You know how when you don't want to go to work and you call in sick? Then someone from work calls and you fake a cough or try to sound miserable."

"I've done that."

"Think we all have."

"You think that's what Wagner's doing?"

"Could be. If you're right about him conducting a private investigation and he doesn't want anyone to know. The question is—"

"Why is he doing it? Is he after the sheriff or is he the bad guy?"

"Exactly. Hopefully, Jen'll dig up something useful one way or another. Meanwhile, I think we should birddog Wagner and see what he's up to."

"I can do that."

"No. You've been up all night. I'll do it. I'd like you to stay here with Tessa and Paula though. I don't think they'll take off or contact anyone, but I'll feel better if one of us is with them. And try to get some rest. You can use our bed. There are clean sheets in the linen closet in the bedroom if you want."

"Okay, thanks."

"You need this computer?"

"No. I've got my iPad."

I bluetoothed photos of Wagner and his truck to my phone, gave Barb back her SD card, told her our Wi-Fi network name and password and shut down. I got my stuff together and went to check on Tessa and Paula.

When I first bought the condo, our personal gym had been a second master bedroom with floor to ceiling windows and sliding glass doors looking out at the river. My then lover and partner in life, Karen Tanaka, turned it into her art studio with a linoleum floor. Then Karen suddenly disappeared and I didn't know why until a year later when I discovered she'd been murdered. I found and killed her killer. After Wendy moved in with me, we converted the room to a gym rather than turning it back into a bedroom or keeping it as a shrine to Karen as I had been doing.

Karen will always be a part of me, a part of our lives but an appropriate part. Several of her paintings decorate the condo. Her picture with her impish smile sits among our family photos. Though often, when I go to our gym, I'll get a catch in my throat and my vision will blur and I'll see Karen working furiously at her easel, barefoot, naked to the waist in a paint-spattered pair of pants.

Tessa and Paula were staring out the windows as they worked out. Tessa had changed back into sweats and was wearing earbuds while jogging on the treadmill. Paula rowed steadily in place on the rowing machine. I moved to where they could see me. They stopped and Tessa removed an earbud.

"I need to check on some developments. Barb is here if you need anything. She has the password to our Wi-Fi and there's lots of stuff on TV or books. There's plenty of food and drink. Help yourselves. Please don't go out and please don't tell anyone where you are. It's not safe. Please don't answer the phone or door. We're the only ones except Carmen who know you're here. Let's keep it that way, okay?"

"Can I go with you?"

"Tessa, that's not a good idea."

"But I wanna help."

"I understand that, and you've already helped a great deal."

"But I *wanna* do more. He killed my family. I have the right—"

"You have the right to see him prosecuted and convicted. Your testimony will help do that. You're very brave but you're also in danger. Sorry. You're safer here."

"She's right, Tess."

Tessa left the room in a huff.

"She knows you're right."

"I can't take the chance she'll get hurt or do something stupid."

"I know. She'll get over it."

"I understand her feelings. Wanting to get back at whoever killed someone you loved. I've been there. Clint Eastwood said something like, 'killing isn't easy.' It haunts you forever. She doesn't deserve that."

"I'll watch her."

"Thanks. See you later."

Barb was in the kitchen finishing the coffee.

"I saw Tessa stomp past."

"She's pissed I won't take her with me."

"Not a good idea."

"Definitely not. Come here."

I led Barb to the front door and pointed to a key in a lock set in the doorframe about head high. There was a similar lock at knee level.

"These are extra security I installed years ago. Don't ask why. They don't show from the outside. You and Paula are exhausted. I don't trust Tessa not to sneak out if you guys fall asleep. Lock them after I leave and keep the key with you. There's no reason to answer our phone or door. We're not expecting anyone or anything. I'll call your phone to let you know I'm back."

"Okay."

"If someone does show up and you're curious, the video display will show who's at the building entry or outside in the hall."

"I didn't realize you and Wendy were so paranoid."

I smiled. "Trust me. It's not paranoia after you've been shot at when opening your door. Call you later."

Jennifer found a list of attendees and vendors for the NSA conference that also included the Police Officers' Association of Nebraska members. She set up programs to locate official and private websites as well as social media accounts of those attendees and vendors that might have posted photographs of the conference and then transfer those photos to another program using facial recognition software to locate Sheriff Donahue.

It wasn't a foolproof system. Many—if not most—of the photos wouldn't be date-stamped. It would be sheer luck if any contained Donahue. It would be miraculous if one gave him an alibi for the time of the murders. Still, it was a start and the computers would be doing the work, not her.

Using her beta program, Jennifer hacked into the security systems of the Younes Conference Center and La Quinta Inn in Kearney and downloaded archived video footage for

October 8 and also ran that against the facial recognition software.

While those programs ran, Jennifer did a background check on Chief Deputy Harold Wagner then went back into the Blank County Sheriff's Department network using the same open portal she'd found earlier. She searched the financial department's records to see if Donahue had submitted an expense report for the conference. No report had been entered as yet.

Unperturbed but curious, she scanned through Donahue's personnel history. Prior to being elected sheriff, Donahue had been a Sheriff-Investigator earning $23.82 an hour and averaging 50-hour weeks. She did a quick mental calculation.

Wow. With overtime, he made more as an investigator than he does with his sheriff's salary. Probably with less stress too. That's what I call dedication. Sometimes it pays not to be boss.

Looking further, she found a 14-month gap in his employment 2013-2014 with the single entry, NE NAT GRD DEPLOY. There were similar entries for 2006 and 2011.

A dinging sound told Jennifer the Wagner background check was complete. Before exiting the sheriff department network, she took a quick look at Wagner's personnel file. Like the sheriff, Wagner was salaried, and as chief deputy he earned $2,483.20 bi-weekly. Her eyes widened when scrolling down she saw the same employment gap as Donahue's for 2013-2014: NE NAT GRD DEPLOY.

Jennifer shook her head. She wasn't sure how long she sat there staring at the screen. She eased out of the network carefully removing any traces she'd been there and sat back.

Wagner was in Afghanistan too. He could have known about the money. He—

Jennifer heard a noise. She rolled her chair back to see what it was. The office outer door handle rattled making the same sound again. There was a knock at the door.

Twenty-Four

When I got to my car, I called the Holiday Inn Express and asked for Harold Wagner. There was little point driving out there to watch him if he wasn't there. I planned to hang up if he answered. After a moment, the hotel clerk said there wasn't anyone registered by that name. He suggested I try the Days Inn or America's Best Value Inn, which were nearby.

I trusted Barb being right, but called the others on the off chance. Wagner wasn't registered at any of them. So where was he?

I drove out and circled the parking lots of all three hotels as well as a Denny's and Cracker Barrel and the lots across the street at Westbrook Mall. No sign of Wagner's truck. Still trusting Barb, I went back to the Holiday Inn and went to the desk.

"I'm looking for this man. He may not be using his real name."

I showed the clerk the photo of Wagner on my phone at the same time I laid my PI license on the counter with a $20 bill under it. The clerk looked at my license, looked at the photo, looked around and looked again at my license. The $20 disappeared from the counter. The clerk consulted his monitor.

"That's Mr. Crockett. Room 327. But I saw him leave half an hour ago."

"First name?"

"David."

"How long is he staying?"

The clerk looked around but didn't say anything. I put another twenty on the counter and it disappeared too.

"He's booked until Sunday. Checkout's at eleven."

"Thanks."

I went back to my car. *Davy Crockett.* Cute. Why was Wagner using an alias? Did he have fake ID and a credit card in that name? Why? Before I came to any conclusions, my phone rang. I didn't recognize the number but it had a 531 area code.

"This is Rachel."

"Mornin'. Baxter Donahue."

"Good morning, sheriff. It's still early. I'm afraid I don't have any updates for you yet."

"Don't worry about it. As my predecessor taught me years ago, events come together at their own speed. Don't try to force 'em. The reason I called is, I thought I could buy you breakfast, if you haven't eaten, and we could go over some things in your report and what I've gotten from Deb and Joe."

I didn't need another breakfast, but I might find out more of what and who the sheriff really was.

"Sounds good. Where would you like to meet?"

"How 'bout Amigos, if that's not too far out of the way?"

"That'll be fine. See you in about thirty minutes." If I make every light and don't get stopped for speeding.

I pulled into the parking lot at Amigos 29 minutes later with no flashing lights on my tail and parked next to a Chevy Tahoe. Amigos is a family-owned and run restaurant that I discovered, like so many others over the years, during an investigation. Sleuthing, good food and I just seem to go together.

I saw Sheriff Donahue sitting in a booth as I entered. I would have preferred a table with chairs as the gun tucked behind my back gets uncomfortable pressed against a booth's solid backrest. He got up as I came over. There were chips and salsa on the table and he was having coffee.

"Thank you for meeting me."

"Thank you for inviting me."

We sat and I looked at the menu as the waitress came over. Donahue ordered *Huevos con Chorizo* with home-fried potatoes and corn tortillas. I wasn't really hungry but ordered a shrimp quesadilla anyway and coffee and water.

"What was it you wanted to go over?"

Donahue picked up my report from the bench and opened it.

"Spoke with Deb and Joe last night. They got a trace on that tweet Tessa sent."

"That was quick."

"Yes, it was. And Deb called again this morning shortly before I called you. That tweet came from a library here in town, and Deb spoke with them when they opened this morning. Guess what?"

Our waitress arrived with our order just at that moment saving me from answering immediately. My quesadilla looked and smelled great, but I was even less hungry than I had been. Donahue's stare and canary-feathered grin didn't help either. Damn, I hate getting caught in a lie.

"Let me ask you something first, Sheriff."

I sat back as casually as I could considering the lump pressing at the small of my back.

"Where were you October eighth?"

"What?

"Where were you October eighth? It's a simple question."

"Where is this coming from? You trying to change the subject?"

"Not at all. It's the basis for the subject. Where were you?"

He sat back and his eyes narrowed.

"Do you suspect *me* of killing my friends?"

"A witness says you were there at the time of the killings."

"A witness? You mean Tessa Ryker? You found her? Spoke with her? Is she all right?"

"Please answer my question."

"I don't believe this. So, she was there, is that what you're saying? Where is she?"

"You haven't answered the question."

"I hired you to find her. Tell me where she is."

"Answer the question first."

"Damn, you're a stubborn woman."

"Yes, I am."

"I was in Kearney. Nebraska. At our annual NSA conference from the sixth through early afternoon on the ninth when I got called about the murders. So if she saw who did it, it wasn't me."

"I go to professional conferences. They're easy to walk away from for several hours and not be missed. Can you prove you were there at the time of the murders?"

He covered his mouth with his hand squeezing his lips together. I wasn't sure if he was thinking or fuming. He pulled out his phone and began tapping.

"The eighth was a Tuesday. I think that was lunch-on-your-own day. Some of us went across the street to a burger joint. I paid with my credit card. Here it is."

He showed me his current credit card transactions for the month and pointed to the eighth. There were two entries: one at Perkins Restaurant & Bakery and the other at Angus Burgers & Shakes.

"Okay. You ate twice that day, but those don't tell me when. You have receipts?"

"Hell no. I filed them with my expense report. I don't carry—have you any idea how far it is from Kearney to Hartfield?"

"About three hours if you don't speed."

That set him back a moment.

"You been checking on me?"

"When someone tells me my client is a killer, damn straight I'm gonna check on him."

"Tessa says I killed her family? That's wrong. I need to talk to her."

"Not before you prove where you were that day."

"I could have you arrested for impeding an investigation."

"True, but that won't get you Tessa Ryker."

He sighed deeply and scrolled through his phone again. He turned it toward me.

"Call this number and put it on speaker when they answer."

The number was in area code 308. I took out my phone and tapped it in. When it started ringing, I put it on speaker.

"Butte County Sheriff's Department. How may I help you?"

Donahue leaned forward and I held the phone toward him.

"This is Sheriff Donahue from Blank County. Is your sheriff in?"

"One moment please."

"Hey, Bax. How you doin'? You found that missing girl yet?"

"Still working on it, Tammy. Need your help for a moment."

"Sure. What can I do you for?"

"At the NSA conference, do you remember when and where we had lunch on the eighth?"

"What's the matter Bax? You lose your receipt or gettin' senile all of a sudden?"

"Neither, I hope. Just trying to prove something to someone. Help me out here, pardner."

"Okay, I'll humor you. Let's see. The eighth? That was lunch-on-our-own because the Police Officers' Association were having a private luncheon, wasn't it?"

"That's right."

"That's easy. We went to that Angus Burgers place. Think I gained five pounds right then and there. Dang. Remembering that Nebraska Farmer Burger makes me hungry all over again."

"You and me both. What time were we there?"

"Must of been just after noon. I remember we were a bit late getting back for the next session the food was so good. Anyway, that do it for ya?"

Donahue looked at me and I nodded.

"That'll do it. Thank you, Tammy. You're a life saver."

"Any time. You'll have to tell me what this is all about some time."

"I surely will. Probably be worth a good laugh by then. Thanks, again."

I hung up and laid my phone on the table.

"Do you believe now I couldn't have been at the Ryker farm?"

"Sorry, Sheriff. I needed to know."

"Uh-huh. Where's Tessa?"

"I have another question."

"Don't push me too far, Ms. Cord."

"I'll try not to, Sheriff Donahue. What did you drive to the conference?"

He stared at me for nearly a minute.

"My old Tahoe. Same one that's sittin' outside right now. Why?"

"Where was your official vehicle while you were at the conference?"

He paused a long time.

"It should have been in my spot at the department unless it was needed because another vehicle was disabled. Are you suggesting Tessa saw my SUV that day?"

I nodded. "She was too far away to recognize the man that came out of her house, but she recognized the SUV. Something about a special decal."

"My name on the front fenders."

"Do you know where your chief deputy is right now?"

"Now you wait just a damn minute."

I picked up my phone, opened the photo of Wagner at Belle's and showed it to the sheriff.

"This was taken this morning. He's here in the city and registered at the Holiday Inn Express under an assumed name. Why do you think that is?"

He stared at the photo.

"I need to make a call."

I didn't care for the look he gave me as he made his call. Apparently no one answered as he hung up and called a different number.

"Yeah, Joe, it's me. Where's Deb? . . . No, you can't. I need to speak with her . . . Only her . . . Well tell her to get off the pot . . . Just take her the damn phone then, will ya. I need to speak with her now . . . Yes, it's urgent."

Donahue closed and opened his eyes as he waited.

"Deb . . . Deb . . . Will you please stop and listen? . . . All right, I'm sorry I had Joe go in the *Ladies* but this is serious. Are you alone? . . . All right. Just simmer down and listen. I need you to go to Wagner's and verify he's sick in bed . . . I know that you told me he was, but . . . Yes, go out there right now . . . No, don't call him or his house and make sure you see him. Don't take Geena's word for it. See him. No excuses . . . I don't know, make up something . . . Just do it and call me back immediately . . . I'll explain when you call back . . . No. Don't tell anyone where you're going or why . . . Not even Joe . . . I said I'd explain. Just do it. Trust me, it's important . . . Thank you . . . Me too. See you soon."

He blushed a little at the end, hung up and looked down at his plate of food, which was getting cold, then back at me.

"I hate this."

"Why Detective Anderson? Why shouldn't she tell her partner?"

"Because you said Tessa saw a man driving my SUV. Till I find out who, she's the only one I'm going to trust. No more talk. No questions till she calls back."

He grabbed a bottle of hot sauce and splashed the potatoes then started eating. He didn't look at me. I picked up a slice of my quesadilla. It was barely warm and the cheese had lost its gooey stretch. Still tasted good. The waitress came and refilled our coffee cups and my water glass.

There was no call before we finished eating. We sat staring at each other across the table. He won when I checked the time on my phone. It had been 20 minutes since he spoke with Det. Anderson. The waitress filled our cups again and left the check. Several more minutes passed before his phone rang and he picked it up.

"Yeah, Deb? . . . Uh-huh. That's what I thought . . . Because I know where he is, that's . . . Look . . . I understand Geena's upset, but we've got bigger problems than . . . Just go back to the office and . . . I know I said I'd explain, but I can't right now . . . Deb . . . Deb, go to the office and check the log on my SUV . . . That's what I said . . . See who used it on the eighth . . . Yes, the eighth . . . I'm afraid so . . . I don't like this any better than you, believe me . . . Right. Talk to no one. Let me know what you find."

The sheriff looked around. Tables and booths were filling.

"Gettin' to be too many ears in here. Why don't we continue this conversation outside?"

He left a tip and paid the check and we headed toward our cars that happened to be parked together. He wasn't happy.

"Last night when I spoke with Debra and Joe, they said Harry left early feeling sick. Joe called him this morning to see how he was. He said he was too sick to come in, was going to stay in bed all weekend to beat whatever it was he caught. Of course we know that isn't true."

He glared at me as if it were my fault.

"Debra says Harry's wife is upset and confused. She doesn't know where he is or why. All he told her was to tell everyone he was sleeping and too sick to talk."

"How well do you know Wagner?"

"Don't you dare suggest what I think you're going to. I've known Harry Wagner ever since I joined the sheriff's department. We've worked together and served together."

"What do you mean 'served together'?"

My phone vibrated then rang. The tone told me I had an urgent text message.

Twenty-Five

There was a second knock and the door handle rattled once more.

That can't be Rachel or Barbara. They have keys. There aren't any appointments. Are there? Doris and Mary would have said something when I arrived. They know I'm here alone, that the office isn't open. They wouldn't send someone down without calling first. If they needed something, they have their own key but they would have called me.

Jennifer reached for the office phone. There was another knock. She called the reception desk. No answer.

Where were Doris and Mary? One of them is always there. A louder knock startled her. Who was it? She tried the reception desk again. Still no answer. If she concentrated, she could just hear the phone ringing down the hallway. She put the phone back.

Jennifer stood. Should she answer the door? See who it was? Tell them they were closed?

She heard a slight scraping. Saw the deadbolt knob jiggle.

Oh, my God! They're trying to break in. Don't panic. Stay calm. Think.

She looked at her monitor array. She put them all on lock screen then quietly walked toward the door. She stood to one side and held the deadbolt knob to keep it from turning.

Outside the door, she heard a man mutter, "C'mon, c'mon, damn it," as she felt him fiddle with the lock. She didn't recognize the voice. He stopped but she didn't hear him walk away. She felt the doorframe shake as she heard a padded thump against the door. She backed away from the door. There was another thump and the door and frame shook again.

Jennifer looked around, thinking. There was another thump. She quickly went to a supply cabinet and took out three nanny cams that looked like hardback books. She turned them on and laid one on Barbara's desk pointed toward the door. She jumped when she heard the doorframe crack.

She quickly laid another camera on the filing cabinets covering the whole office. She grabbed her bag and went into Rachel's office closing and locking the door. She put the third camera on a bookshelf. She went back to the door and listened. She heard the outer office doorframe splinter.

She took her phone from her bag and sent an urgent text message. She took off her shoes and put them in her bag and went to stand by Rachel's exit door. She heard noises and drawers being opened in the outer office. She eased the exit door open and looked out. The hallway was empty.

Jennifer stepped into the hall, closed the door behind her and ran toward the reception desk. No one was there. She ran down the stairs as her phone dinged with an incoming message.

I didn't wait for Donahue's answer. I pulled out my phone and checked the message. It was from Jennifer.

Someone's breaking in!

Shit! I quickly sent back, *Call 911! I'm on my way.*

"I've got to go. Someone's breaking into my office. Jennifer's there alone."

"Let me drive. I have police lights and siren."

Donahue had his Tahoe in gear and siren screeching before I barely had time to buckle up. Traffic was fairly heavy. While he drove, I called 911.

"Nine-One-One. What's your emergency?"

"Intruders are breaking into my office at the Mann Avenue Plaza."

"Are you in your office?"

"No. My—"

"How do you know—"

"My assistant's there. She texted me. She's alone."

"You say intruders are breaking in?"

"That's correct."

"How many are there?"

"I don't know. She didn't say, but she's there alone."

"She's alone?"

"Yes. She needs help. Please hurry."

"Where is your office?"

"It's Confidential Investigations, Mann Avenue Plaza, Twelve-oh-five Mann Avenue, Room Two-twenty-two, second floor, West wing."

"Investigations? Is that a private detective agency?"

"Yes, it is."

Both lanes were blocked at a red light. I heard Donahue's phone ring in his pocket as he drove over the median into the oncoming lane to get around and continue.

"Sorry. Didn't hear your last question."

"Is your assistant armed?"

"No, she isn't." I put my hand on the dash. "Watch out!"

A car pulled out of a driveway. Donahue swerved around it. I glanced at the next street sign. We'd only covered 12 blocks. The dispatcher said something I didn't catch.

"But she's in imminent danger. Hurry. Please."

"A unit is being dispatched right now. What's your assistant's name?"

"Hackett. Jennifer Hackett. White; five-seven; glasses; brown hair in a ponytail; wearing a Cramer College sweatshirt and jeans."

Where are you?"

"On Cutter passing Sixtieth Street."

"Are you driving?"

"What?"

"Are you driving a vehicle?"

"No, I'm a passenger. We're trying to get there as quick as we can."

"For your own safety, stay away from the area. Let law enforcement handle the situation."

"I'm *with* law enforcement, damn it."

I hung up and looked for a street sign. Only 58th Street.

"Can you go any faster?"

"In this traffic? Better to get there than not at all."

"I know. I know. I'm just worried about Jennifer.

Jennifer stopped in the main lobby. She looked around and back up the stairs. She ran outside.

"Ouch!"

She'd stepped on a pebble. She stopped and put on her shoes then checked her phone.

Call 911! I'm on my way.

"Nine-One-One. Do you need police, fire or ambulance service?"

"Police! Quick! Someone broke in. They're here now."

"Where are you?"

"I'm outside. I sneaked out when they broke the door."

"I mean, what's your address?"

"Oh. It's Mann Avenue Plaza. Twelfth and Mann. They're on the second floor. Room Two-twenty-two."

"Is this a business or home?"

"Business. Hurry! It's—We're Confidential Investigations. It's a detective agency."

"Detective . . . Are there weapons on the premises?"

"Uh, I think so, but they're in the safe."

"Are you armed?"

"No, I'm just a computer tech. Please, please hurry."

"Do you know who broke in? How many there are?"

"No."

"Are you in a safe location?"

"I think so. I'm out of the building. Please hurry."

"Police have been notified. They're on their way. What's your name?"

"Jennifer. Jennifer Hackett."

"Okay, Jennifer. Help is on the way. Stay calm. Don't hang up."

"Okay."

"You said you're outside."

"Yes."

"Is there somewhere you can get under cover?"

"Uh . . ."

Jennifer looked quickly around. She didn't want to go back into the building.

"Uh, there's an Office Depot across the street."

"Okay, go there and wait for the police to arrive. Stay on the phone till they get there."

"Okay. Thank you."

As Jennifer walked quickly toward the street, she passed a black pickup truck in a visitor space. She stopped and turned back. The truck was a GMC Denali with Nebraska plates. The same truck she'd seen in the picture Barb took of Wagner.

That's who's in our office. He's—

Jennifer heard something on her phone. She brought it back to her ear.

"Yes, ma'am. I'm on my way to the store now. Thank you."

She lowered the phone, looked back at the building and then the truck.

What if he gets away before the cops get here?

She remembered something she'd seen in a movie. She rummaged in her bag for the Swiss Army knife her adopted father gave her when she started college. She cut the air valves on two of the truck's tires then hurried across the street.

Donahue cut the siren as we made the turn onto 12th Street. I could see my building at the end of the street four blocks away. Everything looked calm, and I didn't see any police cars or hear sirens as we pulled into the visitor lot.

I undid my seatbelt and exited before Donahue completely stopped and headed for the entrance. I heard someone yell my name. I stopped and turned. Jennifer was running across the street. Donahue came around the front of his Tahoe and pointed.

"That's Harry's truck. Why's it here?"

Wagner's truck looked lopsided then I saw it had flat tires. Jennifer ran up.

"Wagner broke in the office. I couldn't find Doris or Mary."

"Are you all right?"

"I think he's looking for the money."

"Are *you* all right?"

"What money?"

We looked at Donahue.

"The money you guys stole in Afghanistan," Jen said.

Donahue looked confused. "What are you talking about?"

Jen turned to me. "Wagner was there too. I just found that out."

"What is she talking about?"

"No time to explain. Jen, is he still up there?"

"I think so. He hasn't come out, but he won't get far when he does." She nodded toward the truck.

"What happened?"

She grinned. "Tommy Lee Jones."

I had no idea what she meant or time to find out.

"Stay here. The police are on their way."

"I know. I called them." She held up her phone. "Oh. I got disconnected."

I headed for the entrance taking out my gun. Donahue caught up and grabbed my arm.

"What is she talking about? What money?"

I pulled my arm free and looked at him. Does he really not know? Is that possible? He and Ryker were close friends. He worked with Wagner.

"Is Jennifer right? Was Wagner in Afghanistan too?"

"Yes, he's a master sergeant. What does that have—"

"Tessa found a duffel bag filled with a couple hundred thousand dollars her father hid."

I turned and started for the entrance, Donahue beside me.

"She thought it must have come from Afghanistan. She believes that's why her family was murdered. The killer wants Tessa because she can ID him. He also wants the money. If it's not you, who does that leave?"

"No way. Harry would never—"

He stopped but I didn't wait for him. I held my gun inside my coat as I entered the lobby. I traded smiles and a nod with a man and woman just leaving. I went carefully up the stairs holding my gun tight to my chest with both hands. I kept to one side so I could see down the hallway as I neared the top.

Was Wagner still in the office? Where were Doris and Mary? The hall was clear.

Twenty-Six

"Hi, Rachel. What's—"

I spun quickly. Mary was sitting behind the counter of the reception station. Her eyes went wide when she saw my gun.

"What's—"

I put a finger to my lips and whispered. "There's an intruder in my office. Where's Doris?"

"City Planning Board meeting."

"Go outside and wait for the police."

I heard hurried steps on the staircase and turned pointing my gun. Donahue came into view and stopped. He had a gun but it was pointed down. We stared at each other. Could I trust him? Maybe he didn't kill the Rykers, but was he a part of it?

He looked and pointed down the hallway. I nodded and lowered my gun.

"Mary. Go now. Quietly."

She grabbed her purse and left. Donahue and I started down the hall, one on each side along the walls. I let him stay a couple paces ahead of me.

As we neared my office doors, light coming into the hallway told me the main door was slightly open. My private entry was closed but light seeped from underneath the door. I pressed an ear to the door and heard drawers and cabinets being opened. I looked at Donahue and pointed to the door.

He nodded, went down the hall beyond the main door, crossed over and came back. He looked through the opening then eased the door further open pointing his gun into the room.

Was he going in? He seemed surprised about the money, but was it only an act? Were they partners? Would he kill Wagner to hide his own involvement? I could hear Wagner still rummaging in my office. I took out my keys to unlock the door. Should I—

"Harry! Can you hear me? It's Baxter Donahue. You better come out."

"Bax? Get in here. I've something to show you."

"Come out, Harry, and with your hands raised."

"Raised? What are you talking about? This Cord woman's been fooling us, Bax. She knows where the girl is. I've got the proof right here."

"Doesn't matter, Harry. Come out. I'm arresting you for killing the Rykers."

"Me? Where'd you get a crazy idea like that?"

"I just talked to Deb, Harry. You drove my SUV on the eighth. You were gone from the office from eleven till two."

"What does that prove?"

"Tessa saw you. Saw you drive away after killing her family. Give it up. It's over."

"The bitch is lying."

"Is she, Harry? We've haven't gotten back all the results from the evidence we sent to Lincoln. We going to find out you were there?"

"Maybe there is. I told Anderson I was sorry I forgot to put on booties and gloves when I searched the place with Olson."

"Yeah, she was pissed you forgetting basic procedure like that. Messing up her crime scene. Now I know why you did it."

"Doesn't prove a damn thing."

"It will. It will. There'll be something. Something with your prints or DNA that can't be explained away."

I called out, "Wagner. Did you wear gloves when you loaded that military M9 you used to kill the Rykers?"

"She makes a good point, Harry. Did you think of that? We've got the gun."

Donahue looked at me and I nodded.

"Give it up, Harry. It's being checked at the crime lab here as we speak. The police will be here any moment. Time to surrender, Harry. Let's go home."

"Don't think I can do that, Bax."

"What was it all about, Harry? Money? I hear there's several hundred thousand involved. From Afghanistan. You guys find a cache on one of your patrols?"

There was no reply.

"Yeah, that's probably what happened. Drug money or a payoff or something. What was there originally? Five hundred, six hundred thousand or more? Was it just the two of you, Harry? And you being acting first sergeant, you arranged to have it sent home with Ryker's stuff after he was wounded?"

"Don't know what you're talking about."

"Sure you do, Harry. I remember now. When Ryker came home, he got the farm paying again pretty quickly and you were suddenly flush. Said you'd inherited it. What happened? You spend all your share or lose it gambling? You like the casinos a lot, don't you? So what happened? Did you need more so badly you threatened Terry for some of his then killed him when he said, 'no'?"

There was a long pause.

"It . . . It wasn't like that."

"No? What was it then, Harry?"

"It was an accident, Bax. An accident. I swear it."

"An accident? You expect me to believe that? Was it an accident, Harry, that you brought an untraceable gun to their home to—what—just scare them? Was it an accident that you shot Caroline twice? An accident that you murdered an eight-year-old girl cowering in a pantry? Bullshit!"

There was another pause before Wagner answered.

"They shouldn't have been there."

"But they were, Harry."

"The girl shouldn't have been there."

"I know."

"I can't go to jail, Bax."

"You don't have a choice, Harry."

There was a longer pause.

"Harry?"

"I do have a choice, Bax. Tell my family I love them. Tell Geena—"

"Harry! Don't—"

Donahue rushed in as a shot exploded in my office. I put my keys in the lock but it was already unlocked. I opened the door raising my gun. Donahue stood in the doorway between the offices looking stunned.

The smell of freshly fired gun was powerful. Wagner lay on the floor against the wall, his gun near him. Blood, brains and skull fragments splattered my wall.

"Freeze! Drop your weapon!"

There's something about someone screaming contradictory orders that tends to short-circuit the brain. Confuses you. Makes you hesitate.

"Police! Drop your weapon!"

I didn't dare turn or look. If he heard the shot, the cop yelling had to be as skittish as I felt. A mere glance could be misinterpreted as a threat. I didn't think my revolver would go off accidentally but just dropping it was anathema. I slowly half-knelt and laid it on the floor then stood raising my hands with fingers spread. Strong hands pulled me backward and threw me down on the hallway floor. There were other commands and sounds, but the knee pressed into my back with what felt like a couple hundred pounds behind it had my full attention. My arms were twisted behind me and I was handcuffed.

Two hours later I was sitting alone in an unused office on the first floor sipping coffee. I would have preferred a tumbler of Glenfiddich and a hot bath, my shoulders and back still ached, but—hey—at least I was no longer cuffed.

My gun had been confiscated—no telling when I'd get that back—and my hands and clothes swabbed for GSR. I'd been cuffed and waiting nearly an hour before someone took my statement. Just my luck I drew Det. Wellborne.

She'd been snarky about my being involved in another shooting and didn't like it when I told her she'd have to talk to Carmen Andrews if she wanted to know where Tessa was. At least she hadn't made me repeat my story more than once and she had removed the handcuffs and sent for coffee. After she left, I made quick calls to Wendy, Carmen and Barb. I also called Jen. She was in tears. It took several minutes convincing her nothing that happened was her fault. I told her to go home and rest and not worry about the office or what was on the computers. It could all wait until tomorrow. I had two messages from Tanya but ignored them.

The door opened and Donahue and Denise Brody came in. He looked tired or sad or both. She handed me back my gun.

"Didn't think I'd see this for several weeks."

She shrugged. "It obviously hadn't been fired and you have a valid carry permit. You're not under arrest. Why mess with needless paperwork?"

I would have said, *petty,* considering Wellborne but was too happy to have it back to care.

"When can I have my office back? I need to get a bio team over to clean."

"Probably several more hours. Sheriff says you have the Ryker murder weapon. That right?"

"Locked in the safe upstairs."

"Sheriff, you want to take possession or have us do it and run tests?"

"Appreciate it if you'd handle it, Lieutenant. My department will cover your costs."

"Let's do it then."

We followed Denise upstairs and Donahue quietly asked if the money was also in the safe.

"Nope."

"Know where it is?"

"Nope."

He dropped back a step as we reached the top. Both Doris and Mary were at the reception desk.

"When the police are done, Rachel," Mary said, "Maintenance will repair your door and Bio-Hazard is on call to come clean the office."

"Thanks, Mary. You okay?"

"I'm fine. I'm just sorry I wasn't here to stop him from breaking in. I was helping Pam down at Darby's."

"That's okay. Thanks."

Donahue and I waited as Denise spoke with the senior investigator in charge. I was logged in to the crime scene and given disposable coveralls, gloves and booties and then the investigator led me through the office to the closet.

Wagner's body had been removed but I wouldn't look where he'd shot himself. My nose and imagination weren't as easily distracted. The lingering scent of gunpowder mixed with a metallic taste and odor of bad meat, bad breath, mothballs and a flowery hint I couldn't define. The sooner I was out of here the better. Bio-Hazard better live up to their reputation or I'd be moving.

The closet doors were open and heavily dusted for fingerprints. Several of the extra clothes Barb and I keep there were on the floor and the rest look manhandled. My safe was also dusted for prints but it didn't look damaged in any way.

I opened the safe and the investigator had his photographer take a picture before I removed the two bags and photos Barb had put there earlier. Fortunately, I didn't see the Mec-Gar magazines so wouldn't need to explain those. I slid the bags into two clear evidence bags he held. Put the photos in another. He closed them and made several notations. I relocked the safe as the photographer took more pictures. We retraced our path out of the office and I removed the disposable clothing, which was put in another bag and tagged. The bags with the photos, murder weapon and clips and I were logged out and the investigator transferred the bags to Denise.

"I'll try to get a rush on these," she said and walked away.

Donahue and I followed. We started down the stairs. I stopped. He stopped a couple steps down and turned back.

"Something wrong?"

"How did you know the murder weapon was untraceable?"

"I don't, but I think it might be. You have any idea how many thousands—tens of thousands, maybe even hundreds of thousands—of pistols, rifles and machine guns we've given our allies in Afghanistan and Iraq since nine-eleven? The Pentagon can only account for maybe half of what they issued or tell you where they are. Then there are the weapons that were either lost or stolen or taken off dead soldiers.

"We would recover some all the time from insurgents we captured or killed. Most were turned in. Some weren't, like I believe this one wasn't. So maybe we'll be able to track it's path, but I won't be surprised if we hit a dead end. That answer your question?"

"Sounds reasonable."

"But you still don't trust me, do you?"

"I really want to, but . . ."

"Yeah, *but*. Guess I'll have to live with your *buts*. You gonna take me to Tessa or not?"

"You'll have to discuss that with her lawyer."

He shook his head and gave me that canary-eating grin.

"You'll have to give me directions."

Twenty-Seven

On the way to Carmen's office, Donahue told me he sent Anderson to inform Wagner's wife of his death and Kern was getting a warrant to search their property. Other than that we didn't talk.

I couldn't read his thoughts or feelings. Couldn't tell if his expression was sadness, anger or just frustration. What would I feel—do—in a similar situation? Prayed I'd never have to find out.

We told Carmen what happened at my office and Donahue said Tessa was no longer a suspect and only a witness as he'd hoped all along.

"That's good to know, Sheriff, but I'd like to hear it from your county attorney before I let you interview her."

"We can do that. Let's get him on the horn."

The county attorney was in court but would call as soon as he was available.

"Sorry for the delay, Sheriff. Would you like some coffee or something else while we wait?"

"No, thank you. I'm fine." His expression was far from fine. "I know where the murder weapon is," he glared at me, "but what I'd like to know is where the money is. It needs to be turned in."

"Why?"

"It's evidence. It belongs to the government."

"Evidence of what?"

"Why Wagner killed the Rykers, of course."

Carmen shook her head. "You're mistaken, Sheriff, and Tessa was wrong. The money didn't come from Afghanistan nor does it belong to the government."

"Are you joking?"

"Not at all. It was her father's money all along."

"Where would Terry get that kind of money?"

"He saved it. For how many years I can't say. At least since his wife first became pregnant, I imagine, if not before. Probably wanted his children to have a good education and start in life."

"That's ridiculous."

"Is it? He was a good farmer, wasn't he? Always made a profit. I admit it wouldn't be easy, but it's possible."

"Why would he hide it? Why not put it in the bank?"

"Not everyone—particularly farmers—is fond of banks. But we can't ask him why because he's dead and so is his wife if she knew. I think Tessa was confused because the money was in an Army duffel bag and she remembered seeing her father hide it after he came home from Afghanistan. That's what she believes and what she told me, told Rachel—who, in turn, told you. That doesn't make it true."

"Then why would Harry kill them, if not for the money?"

"I don't know. We can't ask him, either. He's dead too."

"He confessed."

"Yes and no. From what you and Rachel have said happened, Chief Deputy Wagner confessed to killing the Rykers, but he did not confess to your scenario of finding the money and smuggling it out of Afghanistan. What was it, he said? Something like, 'I don't know what you're talking about,' and 'it wasn't like that.' Is that right?"

Donahue and I looked at each other. He must have been thinking as I was about those minutes in the hallway, about what was being said.

"Carmen's right. He didn't say why he killed them or anything about Afghanistan."

"But the money's the only logical link."

"Logical only because it's a convenient storyline, Sheriff. And only if there was originally a lot more than the two-fifty Tessa has. Can you prove there was more? That it was smuggled from Afghanistan?"

"Not sure. Maybe not."

"And Wagner could have had a dozen reasons for wanting to kill Ryker. We don't know and probably won't know. As for the money, my storyline is it legally belonged to Ryker and is therefore part of Tessa Ryker's inheritance. And I'll do all I can to defend my client's right to keep it. She's lost her whole family. The money can't replace them, but it will get her the help she'll need to get through their loss."

I've seen Carmen sway juries with her arguments. Was she doing that now? Playing the pitiful orphan card this time? Trying to convince me, convince Donahue—

"You make a good point, counselor, but—"

His phone rang and he looked at it.

"It's Detective Anderson. Excuse me a moment, please. Yes, Deb, what's happening? . . . Okay . . . Okay. Where does her sister live? . . . That's good. Let's get them away before too many people find out and the press descends but stay with them . . . Can't your mother watch the boys tonight? . . . It's important . . . The boys are sixteen. They can spend a night alone if need be . . . You know how important it is to interview Geena right now, she's . . . I know she's upset. We all are, but if she'll talk to anyone, she'll talk to you . . . We need to know why Harry . . . Thank you . . . I think tomorrow . . . Not sure, I'm waiting for Wade to call back. He's in court. Did Joe get the warrant? . . . Okay, tell him to go in after you leave with Geena and the kids. They don't need to see that . . . Yes, I'll take care of arranging for Harry's body to be sent home . . . Okay, talk to you later . . . Miss you, too."

Donahue put his phone away.

"Detective Anderson is taking Wagner's wife and kids to a sister in Fort Calhoun. It'll get them away from the chaos and she can interview them there. I need to make some calls. Is there an office I can use until Vanderhorn calls back?"

"Sure. The interview room across the hall is vacant."

"Thanks."

Donahue left and I turned to Carmen.

"You really think you can sell that about the money being Ryker's."

"Why not? It's plausible. Do you know how large the Ryker farm is?"

"No."

"Neither do I, but I did some looking."

Carmen found that the average farm size in Nebraska is nearly a thousand acres and in the country just over 440 acres. Nebraska farms the size of the US average took in between $100,000 and $250,000 last year. If Tessa was right about her father's success as a farmer, I could see where over the years he could have put aside the money she found. I thought the smuggled money angle was a more likely reason for Wagner killing them, but as Carmen pointed out, we'd probably never know and solving that wasn't my problem.

We'd been hired to find Tessa Ryker and we did. Sort of. So she found us first. Either way, mission accomplished. And her wanting the killer caught worked out too. Though I still had a nagging—

Sheriff Donahue came back in.

"The police here won't be releasing Harry's name until I tell them his family's been notified. Told them they're out of town and could take a day or two. They've got no problem with that. Autopsy is being done this afternoon. If there are no complications, they'll release the body and gave me numbers of funeral homes to call."

"I know this must be hard, Sheriff, your colleague killing your friends and then himself."

"The hardest part is I don't understand it, and—worse—I might never know for sure. As for the money, I'll go along with your interpretation for Tessa's sake. She deserves it. That is unless we discover proof otherwise."

"I think that's best."

Carmen's intercom buzzed.

"Yes?"

"Mr. Vanderhorn on three."

"Thanks, Jon. Mr. Vanderhorn, thank you for returning our call so quickly. I'm Carmen Andrews and I represent Tessa Ryker. I'm with Sheriff Donahue and have you on speaker."

Donahue gave Vanderhorn a concise report of what happened at my office and Wagner's confession. My contribution was simply agreeing with what Donahue said. Vanderhorn was assured that the police here would provide his office with their complete report on the incident including Donahue's and my full statements and the autopsy results. He agreed there should be no charges against Tessa and said he'd fax that to Carmen right away.

As they discussed details, I left the office and called Barb to give her an update. She said Jen was there and had told everyone what happened.

"How's Tessa handling it?"

"She's in the bedroom crying. Jen and Paula are with her. I'm not sure if she's relieved, disappointed or just still angry."

"I need to talk with her then I need you to bring her to Carmen's office."

"Okay. Just a second."

"Ms. Cord?"

"Hi, Tessa. How are you?"

"Is it true? The man who killed Trina, my parents, is dead?"

"Yes, it's true. Chief Deputy Wagner confessed before he died."

"It wasn't Sheriff Donahue? Are you sure?"

"We're sure. The sheriff was two hundred miles away when your family was killed. Ask Jen. She knows."

"It's hard believing Tommy's dad is the killer. Did he say why he killed them? Was it the money?"

"He didn't say. We may never know the real reason. I need you to come to Carmen Andrews' office. You need to make an official statement of what you saw. We'll tell you everything we know and you can call your aunt. You're going home, Tessa."

I met Tessa and Barb outside Carmen's and wasn't surprised Jen and Paula were there too. Except for her sad sunken eyes, Tessa still looked more Terry than Tessa in her jeans, plaid shirt and vest. I asked her for her wallet and removed the Terry Romer ID cards and gave it back to her.

"I'm sure you'll be asked where and how you've been hiding, just avoid saying anything about having any kind of ID. That's for Paula's protection."

Tessa nodded and I gave the cards to Paula.

"I don't care where these came from. I don't want to know but these need to disappear."

"Thanks."

I shrugged. "Who knows? Maybe someday I'll know someone who needs to be someone else."

"If you do, we'll be there to help."

Barb, Jen and Paula waited in the break room as I took Tessa to Carmen's office. Donahue looked surprised when he saw her.

"Damn. You look exactly like your dad when we graduated high school."

There was a long hesitation then Tessa went and buried her face against his chest mumbling something. Donahue held her tightly with tears in his eyes.

Tessa's statement was recorded as well as taken down by Jon Strait one of Carmen's paralegals. Donahue was gentle in his questioning but had her go through several points more than once. When it was over, we told her everything we knew or surmised, and Carmen explained where she thought the money came from. Tessa's face glowed with the relief of knowing that her father wasn't a thief or smuggler. I hoped it was true.

Donahue excused himself to make more calls, and Carmen suggested it was time to see what was in that metal box. Tessa was right about the birth certificates, her dad's Army papers and cash. There was $2,500 in hundreds. There were also property deeds, insurance policies on Ryker, his wife and Tessa and Katrina, and, perhaps most importantly, copies of Terry and Caroline Ryker's wills.

Afterwards, Tessa talked for a long time on the phone with her aunt while I made arrangements to pick up Ryker's truck from the impound lot. We'd be taking it and Tessa home.

It was raining lightly when we departed Saturday morning. Sheriff Donahue towed Wagner's GMC. Carmen and Jon Strait rode with him. Carmen planned to stay as long as necessary to handle Tessa's legal affairs. Tessa, Barb, Jen and Paula were with me in the BMW towing the Ryker F150. Overall, a pleasant drive with a couple stops to stretch and eat, and the weather was fair and in the upper 40s when we pulled into Hartfield.

We checked into the Hartfield Super 8 near downtown. Donahue said he'd call in the morning with an update and wished us a good night.

We met Tessa's Aunt Beckie who was staying there too and Tessa stayed with her. She seemed a caring person. She told Tessa the farmhouse had been totally cleaned. If she'd rather stay in her home, they could do that. Tessa didn't think she ever could. Said she'd always be afraid of seeing her family's bodies lying there.

Would I see Wagner and a blood-splattered wall every time I looked up from my desk? Would I imagine those smells? Maybe I'd have to move after all.

Beckie asked if we were hungry and recommended an Asian fusion place just a few blocks away. I was surprised that such a small town and small restaurant would match anything in the city. The tom kha gai and sushi were outstanding and better than at a lot of fancy places I knew. Crime and death disappeared for a time.

Sunday morning reality returned as Sheriff Donahue took Carmen and me to breakfast. I expected a local cafe but we ended at a private home instead. Turned out to be Det. Anderson's. We met Donahue's son, Jeff, who looked like he'd be as tall as his dad when he reached full growth, and Anderson's son, Micah. The boys finished eating and cleared their places then went off to do what sixteen-year-old boys do on a Sunday morning—play video games.

"If you've been wondering," Donahue said pouring our coffee, "the answer's 'yes' we're a couple. Been seeing each other now for two years."

"Twenty-seven months come November third if anyone's counting," Anderson laughed as she cracked eggs into an iron skillet. "Whole department and half the town are waiting for him to make me an honest woman."

"She's just being stubborn. Doesn't want to let her ex off the hook for the alimony he's paying."

"That and child support ends the day Micah turns eighteen. So don't worry Bax, you've still got a chance if some younger, hotter stud doesn't come along first."

Their levity lasted through breakfast and clean up then turned serious when we moved with more coffee to comfortable chairs in a sunroom.

Anderson talked about her interviews with Wagner's wife, Virginia, and their three children and Det. Kern's search. The children didn't have much to say and couldn't understand why their father died. Didn't want to believe he killed himself.

Virginia—Geena—wasn't ready to accept it either, and she had no idea why Wagner would want to kill the Rykers. She couldn't believe it was about money. She knew he liked to gamble. He'd been doing it a lot more than usual the past year, and she'd been worried about it, but he'd told her he won more often than he lost. She believed him. More importantly, she said, he inherited a large sum from a great aunt. She said Harry handled the finances, but she was sure most was still in the bank.

She was wrong. Det. Kern had gone through Wagner's financial papers. Of four bank accounts, only one—a joint checking account—had much in it. That was mainly because Wagner's salary was direct deposited into it every two weeks.

A joint savings account had a couple thousand, but two money market accounts had only the bare minimum to keep them open. They'd originally been opened four years ago with $100,000 each supposedly from Wagner's inheritance. From the statements, Kern saw how they'd been depleted over the past year and a half. Several credit cards were maxed out with minimum payments being made. A whole life policy had been borrowed against. The only sizable amount of money left was $125,000 in an irrevocable trust for the children.

Among Wagner's papers Kern found a letter from a law firm informing Wagner he was the sole heir of Abelia Drexel Rosewater of Eau Claire, Wisconsin. The letter and an accompanying obituary were four years old. The woman died in hospice at 107. There was no indication in the letter of what Wagner inherited, but this was also shortly after Terry Ryker returned home. Two months later, Wagner opened the money market accounts and set up the trust fund. Kern would try to verify with the law firm whether or not the money was part of Wagner's inheritance.

"You still think the money came from Afghanistan?"

Donahue leaned forward. "Don't know but we need to check the possibility. Haven't found another reason he'd kill Terry and haven't found how else he'd know Terry had a cache."

"*If* he knew Ryker had money," Carmen said.

"Joe found weapons smuggled from Afghanistan and Iraq," Anderson said. "Why not smuggle money too?"

"True, but will you be able to prove that's what happened? Or that Ryker's money and Wagner's came from the same source? The only ones who know are dead. Conjecture based on probability isn't proof."

There were no definitive answers. Anderson finished briefing us.

During his search, Det. Kern discovered four weapons that had been smuggled from Iraq or Afghanistan over the past 15 years where Wagner served tours. Wagner had kept them as souvenirs with cards detailing each weapon and where and when it was found. Kern also found a card for a Beretta M9 found in Iraq but that weapon was missing. Based on the serial number written on the card that was the pistol I gave the police and was currently being tested.

In a garden behind the house, Kern found where Wagner had dug up a potato patch and had buried a bloodied uniform. Testing showed the presence of GSR and the blood was the same type as Terry Ryker. DNA testing would confirm it.

However, nothing about the money or any indication for why the Rykers were murdered was found. Probably never would be Donahue admitted. With the murders solved, he couldn't really justify using more of his department budget just to know why. He looked at me.

"Don't even think it, sheriff. I totally support Carmen's version of where Ryker's money came from and I don't care about Wagner's. I'm not for hire. Why can stay a mystery."

It looked like the whole town came out for the Ryker family funeral despite the cold and promise of snow. There were so many people that the service was held in the high school auditorium. Even then, there must have been a couple hundred people waiting outside.

After the eulogies, prayers and songs sung by the high school choir and Katrina's third grade class, the coffins were loaded on the back of a horse-drawn farm wagon and we walked the quarter mile to the city cemetery. Dark clouds threatened but the city's citizens lined the way in quiet respect.

The graveside ceremony was short. Tessa stood between her Aunt Beckie and Sheriff Donahue, their arms around her as light flurries began to fall.

Rachel Cord Confidential Investigations
Available in paperback and eBook editions

Life's A Bitch. So Am I. (Book 1)*
Rachel Cord seeks a runaway teen and why gay performers are being beaten at Miss Kitty's Kathouse Kabaret.

Still A Bitch (Book 2)*
Rachel races through a labyrinth of missing persons, buried bodies, sex, new love and an ex-lover who may be a serial killer.

Bad Bitch Blues (Book 3)
Life's a crapshoot. We don't know the result until we roll the dice. But what happens when the dice roll says someone wants you dead?

Queen of Tarts (Book 4)
Rachel must face old demons, old prejudices or lose the love of her life.

Hangman's Oak (Short Story)**
Rachel Cord seeks answers to a 68-year-old murder mystery when one of the suspected killers is found hanging from Hangman's Oak.

Where The Hell Is Tessa Ryker? (Book 5)
Fourteen-year-old Tessa Ryker is on the run from the killer of her family and Rachel Cord is hired to find her.

*Audiobook also available. **eBook edition only.

www.ingramcontent.com/pod-product-compliance
Lightning Source LLC
Chambersburg PA
CBHW071502170626
46811CB00007B/2674